Comin Over

MaryJane Passex

Contents

The 40 Watt Club

2⁰¹⁰

Cassie's POV

"Benjamin Sims," I growled into my phone as my cousin's phone went to voicemail......again. I tapped my foot on the concrete sidewalk by the back door of the 40 Watt Club in Athens. I shook my dark hair out of my face.

" If you don't answer this damn phone I'm going to break your nose once I see you. Come let me in!"

I jumped a second later as I heard the back door open and I ended the called. I whirled around to see my cousin standing there with a sheepish look on his face. He shoved his hands in his pockets looking like a little boy who knew he was in trouble instead of several years older than me. I put my hands on my jean clad hips and glared at him.

"Ben!" I snapped stalking over to him. "I've been trying to get a hold of you for twenty minutes. You're the one who wanted me to come to this show."

"I know Cass," he said stepping forward to wrap me in a hug. "I got caught up."

"Flirting probably, "I said pinching his side making him yelp.

"OUCH Cass!" Ben cried out. "Fine, guilty. I was being BG's wingman."

"Please, from what you've told me that man has no problem finding a woman," I muttered pushing him in the door. " I figure the man gets more ass than a toilet seat."

I heard Ben laugh as I followed him further into the backstage part of the club. He'd been on tour so much the last year or so with one of his buddies, who was gaining a name for himself in country music, that I had hardly seen him.

We walked into what would be termed as the green room and I looked around at the group of guys assembled. Ben introduced me to them and I smiled. Ben pulled his drum sticks out of his back pocket and spun one around in his fingers then pointed it at me.

"Thanks for coming Cass," he said with a grin. "Means a lot. I know you are gonna have a blast."

"I'm sure I will Ben," I said returning his grin then laughed at him glaring at me as I tried to reach up and ruffle his mow hawk.

"Dammit," he grumbled reaching up to make sure it was straight. "Don't mess my do up."

I saw the tall man, who was obviously security look at his watch and shake his head.

"Jesse," he called across the room. "Where the hell is he?"

"Quit ya bitching PJ!" I heard answered as a tall guy with a black hat pulled low shuffled past me. He had a tray of shots in his hand and was wearing a wide grin. He made a circle around the guys passing out shots.

He paused in front of me and I blinked as I looked into the sexiest pair of green eyes I had ever seen. I couldn't help but bite my lip at the wide grin that spread across his face.

"Well hello there darlin," he said grinning. I took in the tight black t-shirt, ripped up jeans, chains and boots. He had biker rings on his fingers. So, this is who Ben had been telling me had been termed as the "bad boy of country music".

He switched the tray to one hand and held out a big hand to me. I lifted mine up to shake it and I heard Ben growl beside me when he lifted my hand up to place a soft kiss on the back of my knuckles. Im Brantley. "And who is this lovely angel standing in front of me?"

"Off limits," Ben said pointing a drumstick at him as he passed me a shot to toss back. I took the shot with a wide grin. Ben sighed after I kicked his shin. I was twenty-three years old for crying out loud not a little kid anymore. "BG this is my cousin Cassie. Cass, this is BG."

"Well, it's a pleasure to meet you honey," Brantley drawled before taking his shot and grinning at me. "You sticking around for the show?"

"Yep," I said giving him a flirty smile and throwing an elbow in Ben's ribs. "I promised this jackass I would before I have to catch a flight later."

"Flight?" he murmured stepping closer to me. "Where to?"

"Wouldn't you like to know?" I answered with a wink.

"I'd be down to finding out after the show," he said looking into my eyes. I could hear Ben groan as the guy I had been introduced to as Jesse started laughing. I heard another voice call out and jumped breaking his stare.

"Alright boys," the man said. Its time.

"Well, time to go to work darlin," Brantley said giving me a soft smile and squeezing my hand one more time. I jumped with the spark I felt. Damn. I had just met this man and he made my knees week. He turned and headed towards the door with the other guys following him. Ben looped an arm around my shoulders and kissed the top of my head and pointed at PJ.

"Stick close to PJ and he will keep an eye on you if you want to be down close to the stage Cass," he said with a smile.

"Sounds good," I said returning his smile. "Kick ass."

"Always!" Ben called over his shoulder as he jogged towards the stage.

"Ready Cassie?" PJ asked giving me a grin. I nodded and started to follow him.

"Ready as I will ever be," I answered with a laugh. "Ben has told me it can get kind of rowdy."

"Yes mam," he said with a booming laugh as he pointed to an open spot to the side of the stage. "It can."

I made my way to lean against the stage and jumped when a booming guitar rift kicked off as Ben started pounding on his drums. Lord, he looked awesome up there. I was proud of him. He'd sent me the CD's for Brantley I just hadn't really slowed down to listen to them yet all the way through.

Man was talented I knew that. Not to mention hot as hell. I watched Brantley run around the stage and was amazed at the mans energy. They wrapped up the song and he was handed a guitar. With a nod at Ben he started to strum. I got lost watching his hands expertly play the strings. I was mesmerized listening to his voice live.

She says

"Look baby I'm a rock star"

Grabs my old guitar

Playin' it upside down

Dancin' around

In front of our TV

I can't see the ballgame

So I just wave my lighter and say

Yeah, rock on baby

I'd rather watch you anyway

But when you're done

Can I come backstage

And get you to sign your name

On that Zeppelin shirt of mine you're wearin'

I'll never wash that thing again

I couldn't help it my heart skipped a beat as he opened his eyes and turned his head slightly to lock eyes with me. Brantley slung his guitar around to his back. He gave me a wink before launching into the chorus and picking his mic up off the stand and walking towards me. My eyes grew wide as he squatted down and reached for my hand and sang the chorus looking into my eyes.

Yeah but she's my kinda crazy

The little games she plays

Lord they'll never get old

She's too cute to get on my last nerve

The way she throws her little fits

Pokin' out her lip and bitin' mine when we kiss

There ain't a fight that she can't win

That's my baby

And she's my kinda crazy

He gave me another wink and blew a kiss at me before moving back to the middle of the stage. Every so often his eyes would drift towards mine and I noticed a couple girls standing in front of the middle of the stage give me dirty looks. I shrugged at one redhead and lifted my eyebrow in challenge.

I can't help it if I seemed to have caught the man's attention for the night. I had a on a fitted black t-shirt that had CASH written on the front in big white letters with a pair of tight jeans and my boots. I knew I had to catch a plan out for an audition in a few hours so I hadn't been overly worried about what I looked like tonight. At least all of my assets were covered.......unlike some people.

After The Show

I walked off the stage after an encore grinning like a fool. I could not shake the sight of the raven haired beauty with the chocolate brown eyes that had walked in with Ben before we took the stage. My eyes the whole night hadn't strayed far from her. She was knock your socks off stunning without even trying. I'd had to hide behind my guitar a time or two on stage thinking about those long legs of hers.

Jesus, they took my breath away just in a pair of tight jeans. I took a long drink of the beer that had been handed to me as I walked off stage and looked around for her. So, she was Ben's cousin that was like a sister to him. I knew I probably shouldn't cross that line but I'll be damned, I had to know her. I stopped in my tracks and frowned for a moment at a realization.

Since laying eyes on her backstage, I'd only had a few shots of whiskey with the guys and a couple of beers throughout our set. I hadn't even thought about Amber or taking a pill at all. Damn, who was this girl and why did I feel like I was hooked. All I did was shake her damn hand. Ok, ok, I flirted while I was on stage and sang to her. Nope, not happening. I may flirt a little and see if I can take it to more. But other than a night, shit that was it.

Ben gave me a wink as he walked by twirling a drum stick in his hand before making a beeline to the blonde in a short skirt he had been talking to before the show. Jesse clapped me on the shoulder as he walked by to grab a beer and take a seat. I knew we were due to get back on the road tomorrow. Think the next show was somewhere in Texas. I'd have to check with Jeff.

I ran a hand down my face then took another pull from my beer. I reached up to turn my hat around backwards scanning the room a little disappointed. Hmmm...... I guess she left. Dammit. Then I noticed PJ walking in out of the corner of my eye and couldnt help the wide grin that spread across my lips as I noticed Cassie trailing behind him.

She glanced over at Ben, who was grinning down at the big boobed blonde and rolled her eyes. Then she looked over and locked eyes with me as a small smile formed on her pink lips. I threw my shoulders back and puffed my chest out a little bit and strode over to her.

"Hey," I said stopping in front of her. She pushed a dark strand of hair behind her ear and gave me a smile.

"Hey yourself," she said back with a laugh. She shifted on her feet a little and licked her lips. Oh, fuck me. I wanted nothing more than to lick them for her. I must have been staring because the next thing I knew she was snapping her fingers in front of my face laughing. "Earth to BG! Come in BG!"

I shook my head and was glad the light in the room wasn't all that bright because I could feel my cheeks grow a little pink. What the hell! I haven't blushed over a girl since high school!

"Umm....." I mumbled trying to get a grip on myself as her brown eyes twinkled with laughter. "Can I get you anything to drink?"

"No," she said giving me a soft smile. "I'm good, but thank you though. I have to head to the airport later. Ben said y'all are headed to Texas next?"

"Yea," I said pointing towards a corner of the room and placing a hand on the small of her back to get to follow me. "I think we are getting on the road around two tomorrow afternoon."

"Ah lucky you," Cassie said turning to lean her back against the wall looking up at me. "Ben had sent me your CD's and I've listened to a few songs. I did hear a couple tonight I'm familiar with that have been on the radio."

"Really?" I asked leaning my shoulder against the wall and facing her. "Which ones were those?"

"Dirt Road Anthem" and "My Kinda Party", she said crossing her arms across her t-shirt covered chest. I was trying really hard to not try and get a good judge at what was lying underneath CASH. "I know Jason Aldean put those out. You did a really good cover of them."

I couldn't help the cocky smirk that spread across my lips but dialed it down as I leaned closer to her. "Darlin, those weren't covers. I have been singing both of those songs for a while. I cowrote "Dirt Road Anthem" and wrote "My Kinda Party".

"Well aren't you just a man of many talents," Cassie said with the sexiest damn giggle I have ever heard and gave me a grin. "Nice job there".

"Well thank ya mam," I said thickening my Georgia drawl even more. "That I am. So where are you from?"

"Here in Athens," she said. "But I travel a lot. How about you?"

"I grew up in Jefferson," I said taking a drink of my beer. "Right now, I'm either on a bus or back and forth between there and Nashville."

"Hey BG!" a voice calls from across the room. I turned my head slightly to look over at a brunette and two of her other friends talking to John. "The girls here want to know..boxers or briefs?"

I gave Cassie a slight grin as she shook her head and laughed. "Nottthhh hiiinnnnnn....." I replied earning a squeal from the three girls. I turned my head to look back down at Cassie and gave her a wink as I leaned forward to whisper close to her ear. I got a wiff of her perfume and stifled a groan. She smelled so damn good. "I'd be glad to show you I'm not lying darlin."

She snorted and placed a small hand into the middle of my chest pushing me back slightly with a grin as she patted. "I'll take your word for it hotshot."

"You sure darlin," I said softly staring down at her and pushing against her hand slightly. I felt her nails dig into my t-shirt grazing my chest and my jeans started to feel a little tight. Hell, what would it be like if I actually got my hands on her. I broke my eyes away from hers as she licked her pink lips again. I just wanted one taste.

"Yep," Cassie said quietly then glancing at her watch. "I am sure. I've got to be going soon anyhow. Catching the red eye to LA."

"Oh," I said softly looking down at my boots to hide my disappointment. Yes, I wanted to get in her pants. I won't lie about that but I was enjoying talking to her too. It was just something about her. "What is it that you do? Still in college huh?"

"Nope," she said shaking her head and stepping a little closer to me. "I guess you will just have to wonder. I've really got to get going Brantley. It was really great to meet you. Was a hell of a show."

She gave my arm a squeeze then stepped around me, her eyes searching the room. I looked around to and noticed Ben and the blonde were nowhere in sight.

"I'll tell him you said bye," I said as she turned her head back to look at me.

"Thanks BG," she murmured and went to walk away. I grabbed her hand to tug her back spinning her around and pushing her back against the wall making her gasp. I glanced into her deep brown eyes for a half a second before lowering my head to brush my lips against her soft ones. I just had to have one taste.

And that one taste right there set my senses on fire. I dropped my empty beer bottle on the floor beside me and tunneled both big hands into her long hair deepening the kiss. Cassie reached her hands up to grip my wrists as I heard a soft moan from her. I was cocked back and ready to go off just one kiss.

I slid my right hand down to grip her hip pulling her closer to me and she kissed me back before pulling her head away. She sucked in a deep breath as she looked up into my eyes. I could see the want there. There had to be other flights. What was stopping her?

"Brantley," she whispered holding a hand up to stop me as I lowered my head to kiss her again. "I've really got to go. I'm sorry."

I bit my lip and tried to hide my disappointment as she gave me a quick hug and darted around me.

"Can I at least have your number?" I asked making her stop mid step. She turned to look at me over her shoulder and gave me a sweet smile followed by a wink.

"Well," she said with a quiet laugh. "If you want it bad enough I guess you can figure it out. See ya later hotshot."

Then with what seemed like a blink she was gone. I reached up to rub my thumb across my lips where I could still taste her before grumbling and going in search of a bottle of Jack. I fell asleep later that night with the vision of a smiling raven haired beauty in my mind.

Ah Ha! I found it!

B rantley's POV

I flip and flopped in my bunk. Turned and punched my pillow and glared at the bunk above me as Jesse snored away. I wish I could sleep. It had been three months since that night in Athens and we were headed back home. I had done everything I could to beg, plead, and borrow to Ben to get Cassie's number.

I had even called his mom and she wouldn't budge either. I had gotten yelled at by Ben and reminded that if Cassie wanted to talk to me she would have already asked him for my number or given it to me that night. Argghhhh.......

I wanted to at least talk to her one more time. I hadn't been able to get her out of my head since that night. Since we were headed home maybe I would run into her again. Hell, I'd comb every bar in Athens if I had to. I tapped my fingers on my chest then grinned as an idea I should have thought of sooner hit me. I pushed the curtain back and carefully eased out of my bunk to creep into the kitchen. I remembered that Ben had plugged his phone up in there earlier.

I spied it sitting on the counter and picked it up as I slid mine out of the pocket. I flipped through his contacts real quick and found what I was looking for. I let out a sigh of relief when I found Cassie's number and programmed it into my phone. It was the beginning of December and we'd be home until the beginning of January before hitting the studio again some.

Maybe I could catch up with her while I was home. I had asked Ben what it was that she did but he had just grinned. I tip toed and crawled back in bed with a big yawn. I knew it was close to four in the morning so I would try and call her tomorrow when I got home.

I took a deep breath the next day around noon as I walked out onto the back deck at Mama's and pulled my phone out of my pocket after lighting a cigarette. I sank down into the rocking chair I had gotten made for her last Christmas with a sigh. I pulled up Cassie's number and debated with myself on calling or texting her.

I shook my head at being chicken. Wasn't like I had any problem finding a girl to hook up with if I wanted to, but I had stayed away from feeling anything for one since Amber walked out and had not come back. Said she couldnt handle the pills and drinking anymore.

Dammit, I had it under control. My finger hovered over the SEND button with hesitation. She seemed like such a good girl. Did I really want to expose her to that side of me? I could keep her as a friend and do my damnedest to keep her away from it. I hit the button and lifted the phone to my ear as it started to ring.

"Hello," I heard a groggy voice come through the phone as I could hear covers rustle around. Damn, I woke her up. "Hellooooo......"

I cleared my throat before talking. "Cassie," I said hearing my voice crack just a little and I winced. Way to go BG. Sound sooooo smooth.

"Yes," she said. I could just see her narrowing her eyes at the phone. What was it about this girl that made me feel like I was fifteen again.

"Hey, ummm this is Brantley," I said tapping my finger on my knee pondering if I could sneak a beer and Mama not kill me. "I met you a couple of months ago when you came to see Ben."

"Oh yea," she said quietly. "Hey, how have you been hotshot?"

"Pretty good," I replied with a chuckle. "We've been busy. Getting a little down time before going back into the studio."

"That's what Ben was telling me the other day," Cassie said. "I see you finally figured out how to get my number."

"Darlin," I said with a laugh. "I have been trying since the day after I met you. Ben wouldn't budge. Said if you had wanted me to have it you would have given it to me."

"Ughhh.... that over protective jackass," she grumbled. "How did you finally get it out of him?"

"Well....." I drawled out with a chuckle and settled back in the chair. "I may have got the number out of his phone early this morning while he was snoozing away. He's kept it close since I had been begging but guess he forgot last night."

"Serves his ass right," Cassie said with a sleepy giggle then a yawn.

"I'm sorry if I woke you up darlin," I said quietly.

"It's fine BG," she said with a quiet laugh. "I didn't get in until early this morning. I've got time off too until around the first of the year. Drove in from the airport and crashed."

"So," I asked my curiosity piqued. "What is it that you do? You already know what I do so it's only fair."

"Promise to not laugh," Cassie said with a chuckle.

"Cross my heart honey," I replied with a smile.

"I'm an actress," she said. "Nothing really big yet. Music videos, a couple of TV shows, commercials, and a few small roles in some smaller movies. But I stay pretty busy."

"Really?" I asked as my eyes widened.

"You said you wouldn't laugh Brantley," she drawled with a chuckle.

"I'm not. I promise," I said shaking my head even though she couldn't see me. "Wasn't what I was expecting. I thought you might go to school out in LA."

"Nope," she said.

"So, um, I know you just got in and we did to, but uh," I stammered. Get it together B. "I'd really like to see you. Would you like to get together and do something later?"

"Brantley," she said slowly. Shit, here it comes I was gonna get turned down. I foresaw a date with a bottle of Jack if that happened. "I'm still a little jet lagged but if you would be down for just watching some movies here I would be up for that."

I fist pumped the air then was glad that no one was around to see it. Kolby would give me so much hell. I was almost twenty-six years old. I cant remember the last time I was excited about a date. Damn, it really had been a while. "Yea darlin. That sounds like a plan to me. Want to text me your address?"

"Yea, I can do that," Cassie said. I couldn't wipe the grin off my face. "I've got plenty of movies. Think I can sweet talk you into pizza, wine, and cookies?"

"Please say chocolate chip darlin," I said biting my lip. "Those are my weakness."

"Mine too," she whispered then laughed. "I'll send you the address and see you in a few hours."

"Sounds like a plan," I said grinning like an idiot. "See you then."

"Bye Brantley," she said before ending the call. I knew with my hectic schedule in the coming year I didn't have time for more than a casual thing and Cassie seemed like the type of girl that deserved more. But that wasn't going to stop me from at least getting to know her.

Cassie's POV

I flopped back onto my pillow shaking my head. What had I just agreed to? I know what my schedule looked like for the next year. My entire January and February was booked solid. I'd be lucky if I saw the state of Georgia before April. Good thing I could always stay with a good friend of mine, Kelsey when I was in LA. I had gotten an email last night about a potential music video in March but I didn't know for who yet since all the details hadnt been ironed out.

I knew Shane said it was someone he hadn't worked with before. I glanced over at my phone sitting beside me on the bed. I had been surprised to hear from him. I had thought for sure that Brantley would have called before now. That's what I get for being coy I guess. That and Ben had told me before he had been kind of playboy since his ex walked away from him a few years ago.

I knew I didn't have time for a boyfriend or any guy right now. But damn could the man kiss. I still caught myself thinking about how soft his lips had been a couple months later. I had gone out to a bar with a few friends one night and was passed a shot of whiskey and automatically was taken back to that kiss with the memory of the faint taste of it on Brantley's lips and tongue.

I let out a groan and flopped my arm over my eyes. I halfway wanted to kill Ben for being an overprotective ass and not giving him my number before now. But at least I had the chance to see him again. I felt a grin spread across my lips as I pushed my hair away from my face. Wasn't hurting anything in getting to know him a little bit. Man was hot as hell and a heck of a kisser.

In My Head

Brantley's POV

I had just climbed back in my truck after picking up the pizza when my phone rang. I looked down at the caller ID to see it was Ben and almost didn't answer it. I huffed out a big sigh and hit the answer button. Lord, he was gonna kill me.

"Ben my man whats up?" I said after the call connected.

"BG," he growled in my ear. "Go through my phone and get Cassie's number huh?"

"Oops," I said pulling out of the parking lot to head to liquor store. Woman said wine and I already had the best damn chocolate chip cookies in the world since Mama had made some homemade earlier. I was looking to impress. "I'm sorry man. Look I just really wanted to talk to her again."

"Just talk huh," Ben muttered. "Pretty sure after she got through reaming my ass a new one for not already giving it to you, she mentioned she had a date with you tonight."

"Yea I am headed that way now," I said taking a right. "She said she was still jet lagged. So just hanging out watching movies and eating pizza."

"BG, I love you like a brother," he said heaving out a big sigh. I pulled into the parking lot of the store and put my truck in park. "But man please, please I am begging you. Don't let Cass be a hit it and quit it."

"Dammit Ben!" I snapped. "I completely understand that she's family. I am being honest. I want to get to know her. All we are doing is hanging out. She's not like the other girls I've had around ok. I know that. I really just want to get to know her. That's all."

"Fine," he grumbled. "But I reserve the right to kick your ass. And man, I hate that I'm saying this, but try and stay sober."

"Ben," I sighed climbing out of my truck. "I'm good I promise. I've got a handle on this but I don't really want her to see that side ok. Plus, I'm picking up wine dude. You know that ain't really my cup of tea."

"Ok," Ben said. "Get anything that is sweet and red and you will be good to go."

"Thanks bro," I said ending the call.

A little bit later I pulled into Cassie's driveway and parked. I put the wrapped plate of cookies on top of the pizza boxes and grabbed the bottle of wine then shut the door to head towards the front door. I took a deep breath as I pushed the doorbell. A minute later I heard footsteps and the door opened.

I bit the inside of my cheek to stifle a gasp as Cassie appeared. Heaven help me she was more beautiful than I remembered. Her raven hair was tousled around her shoulders and she was wearing a black pair of sweatpants with a red long sleeve UGA t-shirt and a pair of red fuzzy socks. She looked adorable.

"Hey," I said giving her a wide smile. She gave me a grin as she stepped to the side to let me in.

"Hey," Cassie said shutting the door behind us as I stopped to look down at her. I stared into her eyes for a moment and shook off the want to kiss her so damn bad.

"Where do you want this?" I asked breaking my gaze.

"In here is fine," she said walking into the living room and pointing at the coffee table after she took the bottle of wine from my hand. I sat the plate and the boxes down before kicking my boots off. "Oh my god Brantley! Are those homemade cookies?"

"Yea," I said with a chuckle as a wide grin spread across her pink lips. "My mama had made some since I came home. I batted my eyes and got her to fix me a plate of them."

"Ahh," she said with a grin as she walked towards the kitchen. "A mama's boy. I don't have any wine glasses. I broke my last one a while back. But I do have coffee cups."

"Guilty," I said with a sheepish grin shrugging my shoulders. I slipped my leather jacket off to sit it on the back of the chair near the couch. "That's fine with me."

She came walking back in a few seconds later carrying a couple coffee cups, plates, and some napkins then pointed at the floor by the couch before sliding down to put her back against it. I tossed my phone and keys onto the table and followed suit. She opened the wine pouring us both some as I loaded us up with pizza.

"Sooooo," I drawled with a grin as she took a big bite. "An actress huh?"

"I told you not to laugh at me," she said glaring over at me playfully.

"Oh no darlin," I said giving her a wink. "I am laughing with you."

I let out a yelp when she pinched my arm and took a sip of her wine. I tried it myself and wasn't too bad. I got so lost looking at her that I didn't even notice it I missed the burn that it wasnt whiskey. "Is it just you living here?"

"Yea," Cassie said with a sad half smile. "I grew up here. My mom and dad died in a car wreck when I was eighteen so it's all mine now. It's home and one of the reasons I won't move to LA full time."

I stretched my hand over to squeeze hers gently. "I'm sorry to hear that darlin."

"It's ok," she said glancing down at the table. "You just learn to live with it. So, how goes the harem of women that follow y'all around? Anyone of them caught your eye?"

"Cassie," I said looking into her brown eyes. "I wouldn't be sitting here if that was the case. There was someone once, but she walked away and isn't coming back."

"Ben has told me a little," she said playing with the crust of her pizza. "Got to remember BG, she's not at the bottle of that bottle."

Well damn, that hit home let me tell you. I sighed and nodded. "I know that."

Cassie was quiet for a moment. "I have to be honest Brantley. With my schedule after the first of the year, I don't have time for too much more than this. I'll be lucky if I make it back to Georgia before April."

"I get it," I said nodding my head. "We are pretty busy too. But Cassie, I'd still like the chance to get to know you."

"I'd like that," she said softly before taking another sip of wine.

We made small talk about our jobs and life of traveling as we ate. She had tons of funny stories about stuff that had happened on set and I gave her some insight on life on the road with the boys. After a while I could tell she was a little tipsy from the wine but she had the biggest smile on her face.

Literally took my breath away watching her. Cassie was just so full of life. She was so damn beautiful and I noticed she didnt have a stich of make up. The smattering of freckles across her nose was so cute as she wrinkled it up at me in humor.

"No!" Cassie said with a loud laugh pushing my shoulder. "You are pulling my leg. Ben did not hit on a man dressed as a woman!"

"I'd swear it on a stack of Bibles honey," I said stretching my arm across the back of the couch and facing her. "We kept telling him but he was so drunk he was swearing that was the most gorgeous blonde he had ever seen."

Cassie let of a snort and covered her mouth with wide eyes as I shook my head reaching up to wrap a strand of silky hair around my finger.

"Oh, you just wait until I see him again," she said with a slight slur. Cassie picked up the wine bottle and topped off her cup shaking her head then reached over to snag a cookie off the plate. I leaned over to grab one for myself and stilled when I heard a low moan slip past her lips. I turned my head slightly to look at Cassie.

She had her eyes closed with a look of ecstasy on her face as she chewed and I swear two things. One, I'd never been more jealous of a damn cookie for bringing that look to her face and two, I'd never look at my mama's cookies the same way ever again.

I could feel my dick stiffening in my jeans and I willed myself to calm down as I grabbed my own cookie. Cassie opened her eyes to look over at me.

"Those are like a slice of heaven," she said with a smile. "Your mama is an angel in the kitchen."

"She's just an angel all around," I said with a chuckle taking another bite. "Has had to be to put up with a hell raiser like me."

"I think you are more of a softy than you want to let on," she said leaning closer to me poking a finger into my t-shirt covered chest. I grabbed her hand in mine with a chuckle looking down at her.

"Maybe," I whispered giving her a wink. "But don't tell anyone"

She let out a giggle and tucked a strand of hair behind her ear. I saw just a little dot of chocolate right at the corner of her mouth. "Cass, you've got something right there."

"Huh," she said rubbing at the wrong side of her lips. "Where?"

"Right here," I said letting go of her hand and leaning closer to rub it away with my thumb as she sucked in a gasp with the contact.

"Brantley...." I heard her murmured as I leaned my head closer to hers as my heartbeat sped up. "If you want to kiss me, go ahead."

I didn't even hesitate in leaning the rest of the way and pressing my lips to hers and wrapping my arm around her shoulders pulling her closer. I choked back a gasp as she pulled back slightly biting my bottom lip before putting her soft lips back against mine. I tugged her over into my lap deepening the kiss as she wrapped her arms around my neck.

Never breaking the kiss, I stretched out of my side tucking her close to me. Cassie snuggled closer to me draping an arm around my waist. She fit perfectly against me. She broke the kiss sucking in a deep breath before looking up at me from under her eyelashes.

"Damn," she whispered. I lifted my hand to brush a strand of hair off her cheek gently. Her cheeks had a light blush across them. "Geez you are good at that."

I let out a chuckle as I slipped my hat off to sit it on the back of the couch. With a slight grin, I leaned my forehead against hers looking into her eyes.

"That's not all I am good at," I murmured placing another soft kiss against her lips making her sigh.

"Oh, I have no doubt about that," she whispered twisting her fingers into my t-shirt. "But I can promise that isn't happening tonight hotshot. I may take you up on that offer one day."

"I'll hold you to that honey," I said leaning over to kiss her again.

A couple of weeks later I shifted my back a little to settle against the pillow under my head and looked up at the stars. Cassie let out a sigh in her sleep settling her head better onto my shoulder before burrowing further into my side with a small shiver. I pulled the blanket up a little higher and wrapped my arms around her tighter.

I had seen her as much as I could here lately. We had come out to Potts to watch the stars. I hadn't done anything like this in years. But damn, it felt good. I wrapped my fingers around the hand twisted into my sweatshirt amazed at how perfectly her little hands fit in mine. We hadn't done anything more than just hang out but I could see myself getting addicted to her.

She was flying out tomorrow afternoon to head to a film location in Montana and we were pulling out for Nashville the next day. I could easily fall for her but I wouldn't let myself. I couldn't give her what she deserved right now, if ever. I had been nursing the hangover from hell this morning after tying one on after finding Ambers ring stuffed in a drawer when I was looking for something.

Mama had given me a chastising look when I had shuffled into the kitchen this morning holding my head and looking for coffee and aspirin. I placed a soft kiss to the top of Cassie's head and willed myself to drift off to sleep. I wanted to do better for her, I just didn't know if I had the strength or want to do it. I couldn't take that leap of faith and get burned again. I knew one thing was for certain as I felt my eyes grow heavy, Cassie was in my head.

Who You Calling Old?

January 2017

Brantley's POV

I stepped out of the shower reaching over for the towel hanging to the side and dried off before wrapping it around my waist and padding over to the sink. I swiped my hand to wipe the fog off and reached for my clippers to trim up my beard.

I was home for the weekend. I'd been out doing radio and press for my new album coming out in a couple of weeks. The tour was kicking off a little bit after that. I glanced towards the mirror and narrowed my eyes. Are you fucking kidding me? I leaned closer looking at my beard. I found three more gray hairs. I was turning thirty-two soon and thats just great. Soooo what I needed this morning since I had already woken up grouchy. I was tired and I hadn't even started to get busy yes.

"CASSANDRA NICOLE PAIGE!!" I yelled glaring at my reflection one last time before turning on my heel to stomp into my bedroom. Cassie was stretched out on her stomach in just my t-shirt scrolling through emails on her phone. I walked over to brace my arms on either side of her.

"Yes, Brantley Keith," she drawled cocking an eyebrow at me. "You bellowed."

I pointed at my beard and growled at her as she bit her lip to keep from laughing. "That's it! We are stopping this shit and getting married! I found three more gray hairs!"

Cassie rolled over on to her back making her dark hair hang like a curtain over the side of the bed and rolled her eyes. "First of all. What a way to ask hotshot? Pretty sure you were a lot sweeter about it the first time you ever asked. We've tried that route remember. Both of us are too damn busy. Doesn't mean we love each other any less."

I scowled at her and shoved away from the bed stomping over to my closet to yank a pair of jeans out then tugged them on throwing the towel over my shoulder after zipping them but leaving them unbuttoned. I walked back out into the bedroom as Cassie sat up to look at me.

"B," she said sweetly. "If it bothers you that bad baby we can go get some dye before you leave again tomorrow night."

I growled and flipped her off which made her crack up. I loved that damn woman to distraction but she could give me a run for my money on being a smart ass some days.

"I'm being serious Cass," I said with a hefty sigh sitting down on the edge of the bed with my back to her. I felt the bed dip as she crawled over on her knees to wrap her arms around my neck nipping my shoulder before burying her nose into the crook of my neck. I lifted my hands to squeeze hers.

"I know you are being serious, she murmured. We tried that road before. Hell, it tore us apart instead of bringing us together."

"But honey," I argued. "Don't you get tired of having two separate places. I know you love this house. That was a couple of years ago Cass. I think we both have grown up a little since then."

"Brantley....." she whined placing a soft kiss on my neck. "Can we please drop this? Our time together is limited this weekend. I really don't want to spend it fighting. And that's all this discussion ever turns in to."I felt her hand slide down to cover my heart. "I know without a shadow of a doubt that right there is mine and mine alone. I know we aren't getting any younger. We are not over the hill yet. Maybe next year ok. Things should be slowed down by then."

I turned my head to look at her. "You always say that honey. And then another role comes up or a tour date gets in the way. I know a way to fix this once and for all," I grumbled.

"What pray tell is that B?" she asked meeting my stare. I leaned my head closer to hers with a smirk.

"I could always just get you pregnant," I said with a wide grin. "You'd have to marry me then."

Cassie blinked at me in shock for a moment her brown eyes wide. Then they narrowed giving me an evil glare. I let out a loud yelp when she grabbed the ear closest to her giving it a big tug and growled.

"I want to see you try Brantley Keith," she muttered tugging a little harder making me lean my head trying to get loose. I swear, she had been around my mama too much. "While we both enjoy the practicing very much, I will neuter you myself if that happens on purpose do you hear me?"

"Yes mam," I gulped as she let go and pushed away from me climbing off the bed. I rubbed my ear and leaned back on my elbows poking my lip out at her as she stopped halfway to the bathroom still glaring at me.

"Don't you dare," Cassie growled looking at me as I batted my eyes at her. "B..... I mean it. Stop with the puppy dog eyes baby."

"But baby girl....." I drawled. "You would look so damn cute."

"I hear that," she said rolling her eyes and putting a hand on her hip. "I'll remind you of this when that does happen Mr. ILikeMySleep. I'll make you get up at three a.m."

I crooked a finger at her biting my lip as she shook her head at me. "Baby, come here."

"Nope," Cassie said shaking her head and inching backwards. "Nuh uh. Don't try to lay the charm on me now mister."

"Honey......" I drawled. "I neeedddd yoooouuu."

"I just bet you do," she said giggling. "I don't know if you can hang. According to you, you're getting old."

"Oh, I'm gonna show you old!" I growled jumping off the bed as Cassie shrieked and took off running. "Get your ass back here baby! I got plans for you!"

"Got to catch me first old man!" Cassie said laughing as I heard her feet hit the top of the stairs. I chuckled darkly and took off after her. I will say this, things were never boring when she was in my life. Problem is, I just couldn't talk her into being in it permanently.

Country Must Be Country Wide: Part I

A pril 2011

Cassie's POV

I stood up off the blanket and stretched when Shane called cut. He'd contacted me a couple months ago about being in a music video he was doing. I'd found out right before I had flown to Tennessee that it was for the next single Brantley was releasing.

I hadnt been able to see him but once since I'd left in January and that was actually catching him in the airport in Dallas while we both had a layover. We talked and texted but that was about it. Even those had slacked off a little. I had gotten the impression from Ben that there had been other girls around. I reminded him that we weren't anything exclusive and that nothing had happened between us so I had no claim on him.

I walked over to Shane with a grin. I had been an extra in a couple other videos he had shot and liked working with him. He never failed to make me laugh.

"Looked good gorgeous," Shane said with a wink as I took the bottle of water handed to me. "Heard you got a part in a pilot."

"Yea," I said with a big grin. "I'm really excited about it."

"That's great Cassie," he said giving my arm a squeeze. "You deserve it."

"Thanks Shane," I said looking around. "So, umm, where are the guys?"

"I think over by the bus hanging out," Shane motioning for a crew member to help him pack up. "Fixing to finish setting up for the concert part and then get that done. Why?"

"BG's drummer Ben," I answered, "he's my cousin and like my big brother. I haven't seen him in a couple months. I didn't tell him I was here. Wanted it to be a surprise."

"Got ya," Shane said nodding his head and checking his phone. "Well they should all be over there and just follow them over when its time. I need you as part of the crowd."

"Sounds good," I said giving him a grin and heading to where I could see the bus parked. I heard laughter as I approached. My eyes zoomed in on Ben sitting in a chair sipping a beer. What in the world had he done to his damn hair? I could hear laughs and giggles coming from the group of girls surrounding Brantley.

He had a beer in his hand and a blonde had her hand on his bicep fluttering her eyes at him. Did one just seriously ask what kind of underwear he wore? I rolled my eyes at myself and her. Can we say desperate sweetheart? Yep, don't go there Cassie. You don't have a claim on the man. His back was to me so I walked over to where Ben was sitting and leaned over to whisper in his ear.

"Did you lose a bet Bennie Boo?" I whispered with a laugh. "You're damn hair is pink."

Ben jerked and jumped up to spin around dropping his beer in the process as he turned to see me.

"Cassie!" he boomed out picking me up spinning me around hugging me tight. I hugged him back with a grin then reached up to push his hair down making him almost drop me to reach up and save his mow hawk. "Dammit Cass. And no, I didn't lose a bet. Just thought it would be cool."

"Okkk..." I said rolling my eyes and smoothing the grey dress I was wearing down. "Whatever you need to tell yourself Ben."

"We told him he looked like a dumbass," Jesse said giving me a hug. "How you been Cassie?"

"Busy as hell," I said leaning against Ben as he wrapped an arm around my shoulders.

"Why didn't you tell me you were coming when I talked to you the other day?" he asked looking down at me. I shrugged my shoulders and noticed Brantley leaning over to whisper into the ear of the brunette on his other side. I shook it off and gave Ben a smile.

"I didn't find out until right before I left who the video was for so I just decided to surprise you," I said shrugging my shoulders. I reached up to rub my arms a little as the late afternoon breeze was starting to turn cooler.

"Well I'm glad to see you," Ben said turning my attention back to him.

"Me too," I said quietly leaning my head against his shoulder. I listened to him and Jesse talk for a minute and I ignored the feeling that someone was staring at me. A second later I realized someone was standing in front of us and I looked up into the pair of green eyes shaded by a black hat that had been haunting me for months.

What worried me for a second, before I tamped it down, was the hazed over look in them, not the crystal clear I was used to seeing. Had things really gotten that bad with him. Yea we talked a lot. But I had felt like Brantley had been pulling away from me some for about the last month or so. I tried to tell myself that it was because we both were extremely busy. He'd been in the studio or on the road so I was usually asleep by the time he was done and he was sleeping by the time I was up.

"Cassie," he said as a half-smile graced his lips.

"Hey BG," I said forcing a smile.

"What are you doing here?" he asked looking down at me. Maybe I could hold out a little hope that he had missed me too.

"Shane had gotten in touch with me to be in the video," I said stepping out from under Ben's arm and wrapping my arms around my waist. I felt the breeze ruffle my wavy ponytail. I couldn't help the goosebumps that popped out along my arms. Ugh, the sundress had been an okay choice earlier.

"Cass," Brantley said placing a hand on my arm. "You cold?"

"Just a little cool," I said shaking my head giving him a smile. He held out a big hand to me with a concerned look on his face. I reached my hand out to his and he laced our fingers together and tugged me behind him as he walked to the bus. I felt all eyes on me and I am pretty sure a few jealous looks from the girls hanging around. I followed Brantley onto the quiet bus.

"Wait right here Cass," he mumbled and dropped my hand to head to the back. I couldn't help but notice he was weaving a little as he walked. I looked around and wrinkled my nose at the bottles, pizza boxes, and was that socks sitting by the microwave? I rolled my eyes. Men, they were just like little boys at times. I heard Brantley's footsteps as he walked back to me. I noticed he had a leather jacket in his hand.

"Brantley, " I said shaking my head as he stepped closer to me. "I'll be fine. I'll just go and change before the next part."

"Or you can put it on Cassie and still have time to hang out with us," he said giving me a smirk. "If I know you, I am pretty sure you are headed back out on a flight tonight."

"You would be right," I said with a sigh biting my lip.

He nodded his head and motioned for me to turn around. I did and gasped as he stepped closer to me. I jerked as I felt his calloused thumb gently rub over his logo that was being used for the video on my neck. He leaned closer to place a soft kiss on it before sliding the jacket over my shoulders. I couldn't help but inhale a deep breath because it smelled just like him.

"I don't know which looks better on you darlin," he murmured close to my ear making my knees tremble with that voice. "My logo or my jacket."

I slipped my arms through the sleeves and leaned back against his chest. I shivered slightly as he pushed my ponytail to the side and buried his face into my neck wrapping his arms around me.

"I've missed you Cassie," I felt him mumble against my skin.

"I've missed you too," I whispered lifting my hands up to squeeze his closing my eyes. I know I could very easily fall for him what little I had been around him. I had been partly putting space between us too. Even if I wasn't so busy, this had the potential to burn me bad.

Brantley gently turned me in his arms to look down at me. I met his gaze biting my lip. I felt a shock all the way down to my toes when he took his thumb to rub slowly on my chin pulling my bottom lip free. I pushed up slightly as he leaned down but the moment before our lips touched a bang sounded on the side of the bus.

"BG!" I could hear Ben yell. "We gotta go!"

"Shit," Brantley muttered stepping back from me.

"It's fine Brantley," I said shaking my head and forcing a bright smile. "Duty calls."

"Yea," he said rubbing the back of his neck. "I guess. How soon after do you have to leave?"

"Right after," I said playing with the sleeves of the jacket. "I have a night shoot tomorrow night."

"Oh," he murmured stepping closer to the door. "Got it."

I saw the brief flicker of disappointment in his eyes before he locked them down. He turned to walk down the steps and out the door. I shoved my hands in the pockets wishing I just had a few days. There had been times the last few months we'd stayed up half the night talking on the phone getting to know each other, but hardly ever had the time to see one another.

I paused at the bottom of the bus steps when I felt my fingers brush against smooth plastic. I pulled it out and my eyes narrowed at the bottle in my hand until I held it up to see the pills inside. My stomach dropped all the way down to my toes. Surely not. I lifted my head to look up and see Brantley standing about fifty feet away talking to Jesse then looking over at me. He stalked towards me when he saw what I was holding. He paled slightly as he pulled the bottle out of my hand then a blank look came over him as he shoved the bottle into this pocket.

"Ready to go?" he said gruffly not meeting my eyes.

"Yea," I whispered calling upon all my skills as an actress to keep the tears at bay. I knew they all drank and partied. But I had no clue about those or didn't pick it up when Ben would talk to me about him worried that Brantley was getting out of hand. I didn't realize it was that bad, he'd hid it from me. "You go on, I'll catch up in just a sec."

He narrowed his eyes and gave me a curt nod of his head before turning on his heel and stalking away. No sooner than he made his way past the rest of the band, the blonde and brunette from earlier latched themselves to an arm each and giggled as he gave them a flirty smile. Well then, I guess I have my answer. I had been doing the right thing in keeping a distance between us.

Country Must Be Country Wide: Part II

B rantley's POV

My whole way walking inside I couldn't get the look that had been on Cassie's face out of my head. I didn't even have to question what it was, it was disappointment. I saw it in my mama's eyes every time I had been home lately. I pushed away from the girls with a quick fake smile and headed to the area behind the stage setup.

I swung and punched the wall even before I realized I had done it. The buzz I'd had going on earlier was fading. If I had just known she was coming I wouldn't have taken the pills earlier, or the several shots of whiskey I had done before she walked up. I thought I had done so well hiding it from her. I leaned forward and dropped my head against the wall. This was why I had been keeping Cassie at arms length.

I didn't want her to see this. Then she fucking finds the bottle I had left in my jacket earlier. I slipped the bottle out of my pocket and shook a couple pills into my palm. I stopped growing angry with myself. This was the problem, I could stop. I could walk away from this. However, I didn't want to. The nights the memories took over and the regrets, I had this as an escape.

That was why I paused in even wanting to try to make a go of things with Cassie. I could have made it a point in between studio sessions to fly to LA and see her. But I never offered. I couldn't allow myself to get close to someone again and then disappoint them.

I still could hear that slamming door echoing in my head. I could still hear Amber's tears and words as she told me she's had enough of this and couldn't do it anymore. I wasn't putting myself in the position to go through that again. I jumped when a hand landed on my shoulder. I whirled around to see PJ standing there with a concerned look on his face.

"You good to go BG?" he asked crossing his arms and looking at me.

"Yep," I muttered tossing the pills back and grabbing a beer as I walked to the stage throwing up the rock on sign with my fingers. "Let's do this!"

I walked on the stage to wait for Shane to give me the go and I scanned the crowd from under my hat looking for Cassie. I finally spotted her standing towards the back of the crowd looking so damn unsure of herself I wanted nothing more than to jump off the stage and run to her. I took two steps then remembered where I was standing and why Cassie looked like that. If I could have kicked my own ass in that moment I would have.

Later on, after Shane had called for a wrap, I eased off the stage with a grin. This had been awesome. This was one of my favorite upbeat songs we had and I was ready to see how it did. I took a deep breath looking around hoping that Cassie would at least come say goodbye before she headed out.

I stood making small talk with Shane as he showed me a couple of takes and we made fun of how pink Ben's hair looked on camera. I looked up when I saw PJ walking to me with a look on his face and narrowed my eyes as he reached me.

"Here," he said quietly handing me my jacket that Cassie had been wearing earlier. I clenched it in my fist then muttered a goodbye to Shane and stormed off. I saw a bottle of Jack sitting on a table near the exit and scooped it up as I stalked to the bus turning the bottle up to make it bubble as I walked.

I made my way onto the quiet bus growing madder by the second and I kept on drinking. She could have at least said goodbye; didn't I at least warrant that courtesy. If nothing else, I had at least thought she and I were friends. I kicked my boots off with a heavy sigh before weaving my way to my bunk to flop down on it. I took another long swig of the whiskey as I slipped my phone out of my pocket.

I pulled up the picture Cassie had sent me a couple of weeks ago from set. She had been headed in to get her hair and makeup done so her hair was up in a ponytail and face bare. She looked so damn beautiful without all of it that it took my breath away. I dropped my phone down beside me as I felt my eyes water a little.

I didn't deserve someone like her and she sure as hell deserved a better man than me. I did my best to kill the rest of that fifth before passing out to sleep that night.

January 2012

I stared into the mirror in the dressing room pale and my heart beating a hundred miles an hour with nerves. You can do this BG, you've got this. I kept telling myself over and over. I had tried to smoke enough cigarettes earlier to help curve the craving to drink something or take something to get through the night that PJ had confiscated my cigarettes.

He had been watching me like a hawk. I slumped down on the couch in the middle of the room dropping my head into my hands bouncing my good leg up and down. I may not be able to run around quite as much tonight but I could still play. I was determined. I liked this feeling better than the high or the hangover from the whiskey.

I'll be damned if I would go back down that road again. My only worry was can I still perform like I had been. I couldn't tell you the last time I had played a show sober but dammit I was tonight. Eric had come by a little bit earlier to check on me and wish me luck. Ben was standing guard at the door along with Jesse giving me a few minutes to get my nerves under control before we hit the stage.

I jerked when I heard a quiet knock at the door. I pushed off the couch to make my way over to the door. Taking a deep breath preparing myself to tell the boys I was good to go I lost all the air in my lungs when I swung the door open and looked down.

"Cassie?" I said in disbelief. I closed my eyes and then slowly opened them again to see her still standing there. She wasn't a dream.

"Hey," she said softly tucking a strand behind her ear and shifting from foot to foot nervously. She had on a loose pair of gray pants with a long sleeve black shirt. Her long hair piled up on the top of her head and an unsure look on her face.

I recovered from my shock to reach out to grab her arm tugging her into the room and shutting the door. She went to walk further into the room but I snagged her hand spinning her around to face me. I cupped a big hand against her cheek and cleared my throat trying to find the words to say.

"Cass," I said softly cupping her cheek grazing it with my thumb slowly as I tried to find the words to say. She leaned closer rubbing her cheek against my palm. "Don't think I am not happy to see you darlin, but what are you doing here?"

"Ben called me," she said looking up into my eyes. "He told me what had been going on. I'm really proud of you Brantley. He said he couldn't shake the feeling that you needed me."

"Cassie, I'm so sorry," I mumbled breaking her gaze. "I.."

Cassie stopped me by laying a finger against my lips then lifting my chin to get me to look at her.

"Brantley," she said looking deep into my eyes. "I am so proud of you."

"Darlin," I whispered leaning my forehead down to hers. "I tried so hard to keep you away from all of it. I didn't want you to see me like that and then you got a good glance anyhow."

"It's in the past, now right?" she said giving me a knowing look. "Ben said you've been sober and determined to make it stick."I nodded my head slowly. "Well then let's take it day by day ok."

"Ok," I whispered letting out a shuddering breath. "Cass, how long are you here for?"

"For the weekend for starters," she said softly wrapping her arms around my neck. "I fly back out Monday morning out of Jackson. But if you want me to be, I'll be back and forth as much as I can."

"Cassie," I said wrapping my arms around her waist as she stepped closer to me. I was lowering my head down when I heard a pounding on the door.

"BG!" Ben called out. "Time to go on man."

"Alright!" I yelled back. "Be there in just a sec."I pulled Cassie closer to me hugging her tightly. The nerves I had been feeling settled some just by her presence." Can we talk about all of this after the show? You'll still be here right?"

"Couldn't drag me away from side stage tonight Brantley," she murmured against my neck. I took a deep breath and nodded my head. I pulled back and slipped my fingers under her chin to lift her head up to lock at me. I stared deep into her chocolate brown eyes as amusement twinkled in them. "If you are gonna kiss me hotshot you better hurry up before the boys barge in here."

I let out a quiet chuckle as I lowered my head to brush my lips against hers. The sparks I felt the moment her lips touched mine shot all the way to my toes. I instantly felt all my nerves settle about performing and suddenly wanted to put on the best show of my career just for her. I broke the kiss with a gasp as Ben banged on the door again.

I gave Cassie another squeeze before dropping my arms and hurrying to the door. I paused with my hand on the door knob and looked back at her over my shoulder.

"You'll really still be here when I get done right?" I just had to ask one more time. Cassie let out a small laugh and rolled her eyes.

"Yes, you crazy man," she said with a smirk making a shooing motion with her hand. "I'll be right by the stage when you walk off later. I'll be the short one standing beside PJ. Now go!"

"Yes mam," I drawled tipping my hat at her with a smirk before pulling door open to see the guys standing there huddled up. I rolled my eyes at them and kept walking. "Y'all gonna stand around with your thumbs up your asses or are we gonna go raise some hell!"

Right Where I Need To Be

Cassie's POV

I followed Brantley onto the bus covering my mouth to hide the wide yawn. I had been on a plane since early this morning. Ben had called me yesterday morning before he headed out to meet the bus asking me to come for the opening weekend of the tour. I had come in briefly for Christmas but had shut him down when he had tried to talk to me about Brantley.

I wished now I had and I would have known what was going on sooner. I had hung up with Ben then got online to schedule a flight. Because of delays I had just made it in time before they took the stage. Throughout his whole set Brantley kept glancing over towards the side to make sure I was still standing there. Poor man, was scared I was going to up and vanish again. I couldn't blame him. It had killed me to walk away like I did the night of the video shoot. But I hadn't known what else to do at the time.

He stopped in the middle of the hallway between the bunks and turned to look at me with uncertainty in his eyes and pointed at the door in the back. "Ben said he put your bag back here earlier. We all figured you would want to sleep back there instead of cramped in one of the bunks."

I stepped forward and wrapped an arm around his waist looking up at him. He'd left his hat off after grabbing a shower before we rolled out and he looked so damn cute without it. "Question is hotshot, do I have to sleep alone or can I sweet talk some snuggles out of you?"

He threw his head back with a laugh then gave me a wink. "I think that can be arranged darlin."

"Good," I said with a smirk dropping my arm and opening the door to find my bag. I pulled out a long sleeve t-shirt and a pair of sleep shorts. "I'll be right back."

I headed to the bathroom to wipe off what little bit of makeup I had left on and changed out my clothes. I walked back out a few minutes later as Ben walked on the bus. He gave me a grin and a nod of his head.

"Night Bennie Boo," I said with a smile. He shook his head at the nickname I had called him for years.

"Night Cass," he said. "And thanks again for coming. He needed you."

I gave him a soft smile before turning on my heel to head into the back room. I shut the door quietly behind me flicking the lock and Brantley glanced up at me from where he was sitting on the side of the bed reading something on his phone. I walked over and placed my hands on his shoulders as he sat the phone down and looked up at me.

"You okay?" I asked reaching my hand up to lightly glide my nails over his hair. He gave me a small smile and nodded his head biting his lip before reaching up to tug me down in his lap winding his arms around me. I settled my head onto his shoulder.

"I will be, "he said quietly after a minute. "I know it's gonna be a day to day battle. But I like this me a lot better."

I wrapped my arms around him hugging him tight. "I'm sorry I walked away like I did that night B," I said quietly.

"Cassie," he sighed. "You did exactly what you needed to do for yourself. But I have to say this darlin, if you are just here because you are worried its not gonna stick or you feel sorr......"

"Brantley," I growled pinching his side making him grunt. "I'm here because I want to be. I missed you. I've been missing you. I've missed talking to you. I've missed the random dumbass texts you would send. I miss staying up to three a.m. talking about anything and everything. I've just plain out missed you, you big dork!"

I smacked his chest lightly as he started laughing. He fell back on the bed taking me with him as he rolled us both to our sides. I snuggled my head under his chin taking a deep breath of that smell I had missed so damn much.

"I missed you too darlin," he murmured pressing a soft kiss to my forehead. I shifted to drape my leg over his hip and pulled my head back to look at him. He sat a big hand on my knee rubbing his thumb softly over it. He glanced down then looked over at me.

"Cass," he said with a grin. "Been laying in the tanning bed?"

"No," I said with a laugh shaking my head. "Been on film location."

"Where are you at right now?" he asked propping up on his other elbow looking down at me.

"I'm done now," I said playing with his necklace. "But I was in Hawaii. I had taken a job for a small part in a couple of episodes of Hawaii Five-O. So even though it's winter here, I got to hit the beach on my down time."

"Oh, good lord," Brantley said rolling his eyes. "My mama loves that show and the main character."

"He's a hottie that's for sure," I said giving him a wink. Brantley narrowed his eyes at me and slid the hand on my hip up slowly and started tickling me before I could stop him.

"Bbbbbbb......sttttoooooopppp...." I got out between giggles as he laughed. I sucked in a big breath when he stopped then gave him a heart stopping smile and a wink. "You're way hotter."

"Good answer," he grumbled with a smirk as he leaned down to brush his lips against mine. I pulled back to yawn.

"Damn," I said blushing. "I'm sorry. It's been a long day."

Brantley gave me a smile and shook his head as he shifted to pull the covers over us. I felt the bus start to move and it took me by surprise for a second. He saw me glancing as I could feel the bus turn and pull out of the parking lot. We were in Arkansas but headed up to Missouri.

"Trust me," he said settling his head against the pillow and laughing at me. "You just used to it. Takes a night or two once we get back on the road but after that I'm fine."

"I normally prefer my bed to not move," I said with a laugh. I glanced over at the clock they had on the shelf and saw it was almost one a.m. I pushed up on my elbow and grinned down at Brantley.

"What?" he asked lifting a hand up to play with the edges of my long hair. I leaned down to put my nose against his making his sleepy smile widen.

"It's after midnight," I whispered my lips inches away from his.

"And......" he whispered back with a half laugh. "Surprisingly I'm still not wired tonight."

I shifted closer to him and brushed my lips softly against his before pulling back a little. "Happy birthday handsome."

He gave me a shy smile and wrapped his arms around me tighter tracing circles with his thumb on my lower back. "Why thank you beautiful," he said shyly. "I have what I wanted for my birthday."

"What's that?" I asked cocking my head to the side looking at his as I played with the chains of his necklace.

"I'm sober, I'm getting to live out my dreams, I have great family and friends who support me," he said leaning closer to me. "And I have you in my arms right now. I'm right where I want to be."

"Well," I drawled stretching back out and snuggling closer into his side. "I told you. I'm here for as long as you want me. I know with our schedules B, this isn't going to be easy, but I want to give it a try."

"We'll figure it out darlin," he murmured as I buried my head into his shoulder and felt my eyes grow heavier. "Day by day and mile by mile. We'll figure something out. But I've got you right where I want you right now and I'm not letting go."

Well....Hello There

M ay 2012

Cassie's POV

I stomped into the dressing room I was sharing with Kelsey. We had met each other a five years ago when I had first come out and started auditioning. She was like me, hadn't had a major break, but we both stayed really busy. We both had been cast in this Lifetime Movie and had been having fun since neither of us had had the traditional college experience.

But the shoots had been long. There was a ton of delays each day because the main star was a total diva. I was beyond tired and frustrated. We had the weekend off. I had planned to fly to Nashville to meet up with Brantley and Ben, but we were delayed from yesterday.

I'd had to cancel my flight out for this morning. B was up there this weekend doing some interviews and theyd planned to catch a show or two down on the strip. I kicked the shoes I was wearing off with a curse.

It had been almost a month since I had seen him and I missed him like crazy. For the most part right now, it had been easier for me to go and meet him. He had been bitching that he hated I was doing all the traveling.

I needed two things right now, some downtime and my boyfriend. I changed out of the outfit I had been wearing and slipped on my favorite robe before walking out and flopping into the makeup chair beside Kelsey as she leaned over to give me a smile.

"You alright over there Cass?" she said shaking her head at my foul mood.

"No," I grumbled as I started to remove the makeup. I glared at the circles I saw under my eyes as I wiped the makeup away.

"Chin up. I know you miss him," Kelsey said giving me a grin and pulling her blonde hair off her face. "I'm gonna go run lines with Alex for an audition I have coming up. If you want we can order some pizza later and unwind. I will help you with the scripts you got yesterday. So damn proud of you for the pilot getting picked up!"

"Thanks Kels," I said giving her a tired grin. She gave me a quick hug before walking out. I heaved out a deep sigh when I was alone again. I started to unwind my hair from the braid it had been twisted into earlier and jumped when I heard a throat clear from the door way. My eyes widened and my heart skipped a beat as I saw who was standing leaned against the door jamb grinning at me.

I followed the trail upwards starting with the tips of black boots, holey faded blue jeans, belt, chains, black tank top, and a backwards black hat. I locked eyes with his green ones in the mirror and jumped out of the chair. I darted across the room and my heart instantly felt ten times lighter at the deep laugh I heard as Brantley fell back against the wall while catching me. He lifted me up to wrap my arms and legs around him grinning at me.

"I take it someone has missed me," he murmured looking deep into my eyes.

"Damn right I did hotshot," I said smiling as he leaned down to brush his lips against mine. "I thought you were supposed to be in Nashville."

He sat me down on to my feet gently to lace our fingers together and tugged me over to the couch in here. I snuggled into his side resting my head on his shoulder.

"I was but when you text me you wouldn't be able to make it," Brantley said rubbing a big hand up and down my back. My bad mood was quickly disappearing. "I begged Rich to reschedule my stuff and jumped on the first flight out here. It was my turn to come to you darlin."

"B," I said lifting my head to look at him. "I don't mind the traveling. I'm used to it."

"Cass," he said with squeezing my hip. "I know you are. But this relationship isn't a one-way street. I can rearrange things to if need be. I missed you. Something just told me that you needed me."

"Awww thank you baby," I murmured kissing his cheek with a smile. It quickly fell and a worried look passed over Brantley's face as tears gathered into my eyes. "Ben told you didn't he."

"Yea," he said brushing the loose dark hair away from my face giving me a sad smile. "He did. One of the reasons he had hoped you would be able to come to us. We could all do something fun to take your mind of it. I know you miss them."

"Six years," I said sniffling. "And I still want to pick the phone up every time I get a new part, or something happens to make me sad."

"I can only imagine baby," he whispered gruffly tightening his grip on me as he picked me up putting me on his lap. "Just don't forget that I am here for you."

"I know you are B," I said softly as he wiped a tear off my cheek. "Damn, I have missed you."

"Trust me," he said kissing me lightly the tracing his lips softly over my cheek down to my neck. "I know. Sometimes talking on the phone makes me miss you more."

"I'm sorry," I whispered. "I should have....." I was cut off when a yelp slipped past my lips as Brantley sank his teeth into my shoulder then lifted his head to narrow his eye at me.

"Cassie," he grumbled. "Don't you dare apologize. Your career is not any less important than mine. There are some things, no matter how busy I have been the last few months, that I can say no to ok. If you need me, there is not an interview or anything like that more important than you."

Sooooo....." I said giving him a sassy smirk and wrapping my arms around his neck. "If I need you during CMA week you will drop it all huh hotshot."

"In a heartbeat baby," he whispered giving me a hard kiss. "Rather be in your arms than walking a red carpet any day. And speaking of that I have a favor to ask of my very beautiful and talented girlfriend."

"Uh oh," I murmured tugging on his necklace. "You are kissing ass so must be a big one."

"The CMT Awards are in a couple of weeks," Brantley said giving me a wide grin. "I would be very grateful if a certain beautiful lady in my life would walk the red carpet with me."

"Awww baby," I said pinching his cheek. "That is so sweet that you are taking your Mama with you. She will be so excited!"

I had been home in March and he'd taken me to meet Mama Becky. Lord, I loved that woman already. I had only really had one boyfriend in the past during high school and we had known each other since kindergarten so I had never really done the whole meet the parents thing. I had stayed too busy since to really date since I had gotten older. She had armed me up giving me a big hug saying she had heard all about me from Brantley and Ben. Then kicked B out of the kitchen so she could get to know me.

"Cass.." he growled pushing me back on the couch as I laughed. He braced his arms on either side of me glaring playfully. "I meant you darlin. Last I checked, your schedule was wide open for a few weeks in June."

"Hmmm..." I said tapping my chin in thought. "I dunno.."

"Cassandra Nicole," Brantley murmured narrowing his eyes at me and sliding his hands down to my sides. He poked his lip out at me making me giggle. "Please baby."

"Welllll...." I said with a smile and patting his cheek. "If you are gonna beg, I guess so."

"I wasn't beggin woman," he grumbled sitting up and pulling me with him. "But if you aren't ready for something like this I get it darlin."

"Brantley," I said standing up to go put my street clothes back on. I paused halfway across the room to look back at him. I am more than ready for it. "This is a part of you. Give me a minute to get dressed and we can head out. I don't want to see this place until Monday night!"

I came back out a few minutes later in the Braves t-shirt, jeans, and flip flops I had worn to set this morning. I was in the middle of pulling my hair up in a messy bun and I paused in the middle of what I was doing to glance over at my smiling boyfriend who was sitting there looking at me.

"What?" I asked finishing up and grabbing my phone and bag as he stood up off the couch to walk over to me. He wrapped an arm around my waist and placed a soft, slow kiss on my lips making me moan in the back of my throat.

"Just thinking how damn lucky I am darlin," he murmured then stepped back lacing around fingers together. We made our way down the hall to the front door of the studio.

"You staying with us B?" I asked leaning into his side as we walked.

"I can," he said looking down at me. "Or I may have gotten Ben to get in touch with Kelsey to send you a bag over to my hotel."

"Even better," I said standing up on my tip toes to kiss his cheek. "Come on. We'll go grab some burgers and I'll show you one of my favorite spots on the beach out here."

"Baby...." I heard him mumble as I stepped away from him to shove open the door. I paused under the awning looking out at the stormy weather that was blowing through. I placed my hand on my forehead and winced. I completely forgot it was supposed to storm all weekend.

"Shit," I muttered. I felt a pair of arms wrap around my waist pulling me back into his chest making me sigh. I needed it this more than I knew.

"Or," he murmured kissing my cheek softly. "We can head back to the hotel, order some take out, and you get some rest. Don't think I cant see how tired you are."

"B..." I whined. Ok, I was a little worn out. Between this movie, starting this new series, and flying back and forth to see him the last couple of months, I was a little tired.

Brantley stepped around me to hold his arm out to flag a taxi down then turned his head to narrow those piercing green eyes at me. Damn, could he look any sexier right now since he was all in protective mode.

"Don't even try to argue Cass," he sighed. I nodded my head and walked up to him to bury my head in his chest. He's right. This right here is what I needed right now.

Cassie Say What????

B rantley's POV

I rolled over onto my back laughing at a story Cassie was telling me about the lead actress in the movie she was working on. She had taken a shower when we made it back to my hotel room earlier winding up in nothing but one of my t-shirts while I had ordered Chinese food. I had traded my jeans and tank top for my sweatpants to get comfortable along with her.

She seemed a little less sad than when I had first gotten here. I had told her we could make plans earlier, but she shot me down saying spending time curled up with me was enough. Her long dark hair had a natural wave to it when she let it air dry. Even in the glitz and glamour of Hollywood, she was still so down to earth. A complete Southern Belle through and through.

"Are you serious?" I asked barking out a laugh as she rolled over facing me.

"Swear on a stack of Bibles," Cassie said shaking her head and grinning. "The poor guy. She proceeds to critique this poor man in front of half the cast on just what he was doing wrong during sex. Like she's some damn expert. Well, she's probably been around the block a time or two. I mean dogged him even down to he wasnt putting his leg the right way."

"Baby," I said with a smirk that made her giggle. "Sometimes it's all about the leg position. Especially when you want to be in control."

Cassie let out a snort and covered her mouth as I laughed along with her. She lifted up on her elbow and looked over at me shrugging her shoulders. "I'll take your word for it babe, because I wouldn't know."

"What?" I asked tugging a strand of loose hair leaning closer to her. "Never been in control."

"No," she said playing with my cross necklace and not meeting my eyes. "That either."

"Cass...." I asked sliding a finger under her chin to make her look at me. "Never done what?"

She flushed bright red and wrinkled her nose. "I've never had sex," she muttered then bit her bottom lip looking up at me. I felt the shock go through my system as I gasped in a deep breath before narrowing my eyes at her.

"Cassandra Nicole Paige," I growled. "Stop fucking with me!"

"I'm not Brantley Keith," she snapped back rolling over onto her back and crossing her arms.

I sat up quickly staring down at my blushing girlfriend shock. No, nah, uh uh. Was she serious? If she was that was scary as shit and hot as hell all rolled into one.

"Cass," I said swallowed deeply. "So, just so I have this straight baby. You are telling me you are a virgin."

"Yes," Cassie snapped covering her eyes with a grimace. "That is exactly what I am telling you jackass. Please don't make a big deal out of it ok. Shocker I know. I'm twenty-four years old and an actress. Kind of a rarity out here. I've kept so busy, I haven't really taken the time to date much, until you. But yes B, other than getting to second base with my high school boyfriend. I'm a virgin!"

"Define second base. Because babe, people have different ideas on what that is," I asked through clenched teeth. I could be about as jealous and territorial as they come and here I was asking my girlfriend to explain to me just how far she had been with another man.

Cassie lifted one hand off her face and glared at me turning as red as my favorite UGA jersey.

"What I mean B," she answered through clenched teeth. "Is other than my shirt being off a couple of times, and some sloppy kisses from my ears to my boobs. Not been a whole lot of action other than self-inflicted going on if you get what I mean."

I couldn't help but look down blankly at Cassie. I had a million thoughts running through my mind at the moment and ninety percent of them were very x-rated. I took in the still damp hair, the long tan legs with bright purple painted toes, and gulped at my black t-shirt that had hung to the tops of her thighs but had ridden up slightly when she rolled over onto her back.

Fucking hell, I had wanted her from the first moment I had laid eyes on her. Literally had thought of nothing during that whole show but how I could get her in bed, but then I talked to her. I didn't think about drinking, taking pills, or Amber that whole night and a few months after when I got her to agree to a date with me. I stared at the smooth tan of her skin one more time.

"Fuck Cass," I squeaked out making her hands drop from her face in surprise. "Ummm..... You're wearing less than that at the moment in some ways because I know for a fact all you have on is my shirt and lace underwear."

"Sooooo observant BG," she grumbled glaring at me. "We are in bed. Not a lot of point wearing clothes to sleep in dumbass." She rolled her eyes at me as she turned on her side to face me.

"You know what I meant Cass," I growled leaning closer to her looking down. "You have spent more time in bed with me since we me than the ex or any movie scene."

"B," she huffed shaking her head. "Think on that. Nine out of ten times its not just us. The guys are close by. You respect me enough to not start anything with them around. So, I've never really thought about it." She pushed up on her elbow to look over at me biting her lip. "It's not that I have never wanted to. Hell, you look at me and I'd climb you like a six-foot tree. The few dates I had slowed down to go on, well they didn't make it past date two because there was just nothing there. I wasn't wasting my time or forcing it just so I could get laid. That's what they make toys for. Now you on the other hand, baby you knocked my socks off with just one kiss."

"Fucking hell Cassie," I murmured leaning my head back against the headboard with a groan running my hand down my face. Blew my mind is an understatement right now. "Baby do you have any earthly idea what you just said is doing to me. You're right I do respect you."

"Brantley," she said looking up at me putting a hand on my leg. I pulled my hand away from my face to look down into her eyes. "It's just sex."

"Baby girl," I muttered shaking my head. "No, it's not just sex. It's a whole lot more than that and you don't even know it. Cass, I love you. I hate to say this, but this shocking revelation of yours changes things. Doesn't change how I feel about you. Definitely doesn't change how much I want you. Makes me want you more actually. Baby, your first time needs to be as special as you are. That first kiss from you blew my mind. Just meeting hanging out with you that first night, I didnt need pills or booze to have fun. I did that just being with you. Sweetheart, I can promise you that when the time comes it's going to be special."

Cassie had sat up so fast after I said those three little words that any other time the thought of them would have sent me screaming into the night. She knew I had issues with commitment. She looked over at me in shock before placing a hand on my cheek. I could see the tears watering in her eyes.

"First of all, B," she asked softly blinking back tears. "Did you just say that you love me?" I nodded slowly as the most heart stopping grin spread across her full lips. "I love you too. And second baby, I don't need anything special. I just need you."

I pulled her closer kissing her deeply as she settled into my side with a sigh. I broke the kiss giving her a soft smile brushing the hair away from her face. "Yes baby. I love you. So damn much. Yes, you do need special because what we are talking about is the most precious thing that you could ever give me. Makes me thank God I got my act together before I lost you forever."

"I'm glad things have worked out Brantley," she murmured against my shoulder placing a soft kiss there. "Because I don't know what I would do if I didn't have you."

"Well, I'm not going anywhere darlin," I said scooting down on the bed taking her with me as she snuggled closer tangling her legs with mine. She was quiet for a minute then I felt her nail trace circles on my bare chest as I stifled a groan. Cassie lifted her head to grin up at me.

"You know B," she said matter of factly. "Doesn't seem fair that I'm wearing a shirt and you aren't."

"Cassie," I sighed shaking my head. "Don't push those buttons tonight please."

"What?" she said with a smart-ass grin and a shrug. "I was just making an observation."

"Yea baby, "I muttered pushing away to sit up. "I know where that supposedly innocent mind of yours was going but if you insist, I will go put one on."

I felt a tight grip on my arm as Cassie yanked me back down beside her with a growl and a laugh. I braced my arms on either side of her head as she tried to pull me closer.

"Nooo....." she muttered. "I was thinking you need to take mine off."

"Cass," I groaned as she trailed a finger down my chest. I grabbed it in my hand and placed a gentle kiss onto her hand. "Darlin. I think it's best if you leave yours on. Not that I don't want to see you baby. I just know that once I start, I won't be able to stop. Because I want nothing more than to show you just how much I love you."

Cassie wrapped her arms around my neck pulling me closer and sinking her teeth into my bottom lip. Holy hell, she was playing with fire.

"What's stopping you B," she whispered against my lips as she pulled back. I closed my eyes and dropped my forehead down onto her shoulder with a sigh.

"Because, I am trying to be the good guy here honey. I only have so much restraint right now and you pressed up against me isn't helping," I mumbled against her skin. I felt the slight shiver go through her body before she let out a loud huff letting me go. She rolled over putting her back to me. I caught a sight of the bottom of her red lace underwear as she yanked the covers up. Fuck!

"Fine....." she drawled getting settled on her pillow. "Guess I will have to spend time with B.O.B. when you fly back out."

I slid over to wrap my body around hers then leaned down to growl in her ear. "I can promise you this baby. When I do get my hands on you......you will throw that damn thing away because you wont need it."

"Yea right," Cassie hugged out with a sigh wiggling her ass against my erection making me hiss out between my teeth.

"Cassie," I sighed tightening my grip where my hand was resting on her hip. "Stop dammit."

"Why?" she whined. "I don't get it. I want you so damn bad B. I can clearly tell that you want me. So why should we wait? Please explain that to me."

"Baby," I murmured nuzzling the side of her neck making her sigh as I placed a soft kiss on her shoulder where my shirt has slipped down. "Have just a little more patience with me please. I don't want you to have any doubts that I am all in. I love you Cassie."

"Ok B," she whispered settling back into my arms and lacing her fingers with mine. "I trust you. I know that you don't just say I love you to anybody. I know that you are all in."

"You're right," I rasped in her ear." I don't. Get some rest darlin. I know you need it." I snuggled closer to her holding her tighter as I felt her breathing start to even out and my eyes grew heavier. I was almost all the way asleep when I heard her mumble sleepily.

"Still don't see why I would need to toss my damn toys away."

How You Doin.....

Cassie's POV

I took a deep breath as I glanced in the mirror one more time. I was an actress I shouldn't be nervous, but oh was I. When your boyfriend was one of the hottest things in country music right now, the thought of walking the red carpet with him made you a little weak in the knees. I leaned forward checking my makeup one more time.

I fought the urge to bite my lip looking at the red dress I had let Kelsey talk me into getting. Showed a lot more leg than I would have liked for my Nashville debut but I'm pretty sure that someone's jaw was gonna drop when he saw it. His reaction was all that mattered to me. I had paired it was glittery high heeled sandals painting my toes a deep red to match. My long black hair was curled and pulled halfway up off my face.

I quietly walked out of the bedroom of our hotel suite to stop at the doorway to lean against it. I smothered a laugh at Brantley pacing back and forth. He looked like he had been at it for a while. He had kept it simple in just his hat, jeans, t-shirt, boots, chains, and leather jacket. I know he was so damn nervous it wasnt funny. He was chewing a piece of gum ninety to nothing to try and keep from smoking.

"Brantley," I said making him look up and trip over his feet as he stopped pacing too quickly. "Babe you ok?"

He stood and stared at me with his mouth wide open. I smoothed my hands down the dress checking to make sure everything was ok because he wasnt saying anything. "What is something wrong with the dress?"

"Fuck no," he said shaking his head and blinking. "Cass, I think you short circuited my brain darlin."

"Do I look ok?" I asked shyly looking at him. Brantley stalked over to wrap both his arms around my waist pulling me close and placing a gentle kiss to the side of my mouth.

"Baby, you look beautiful," he whispered giving me that smirk I knew all to well. "Gorgeous, hot, sexy as hell. Shit, I write songs for a living and I can't come up with words to justify right now. But then again I think you look beautiful in just my t-shirt so what do I know."

"Hmmm," I said with a giggle turning my head to kiss his lips lightly so I wouldn't leave lipstick on him. "I think someone is being a kiss ass."

"Who me?" he said with a wink stepping back to link his fingers with mine. I paused to pick my clutch up off the coffee table and followed him out of the room. "Never."

"Yes you," I laughed pushing his arm as we made our way downstairs.

Brantley helped me climb in the SUV that would take us to the Bridgestone Arena. He placed a hand on my bare knee and looked out the window with his leg bouncing up and down the whole ride.

"B," I said putting my hand on his leg to stop him making him turn his head and look at me. "Breathe baby before you pass out."Rich turned in the front seat and mouthed a quick thank you to me. So I wasn't the only one who thought he was about to pass out.

"I'll be fine Cassie," he mumbled spinning the ring on his thumb around. "Even better if I could have something to take the edge off but yea..... I'm..."

I cut him off by yanking his chin towards me and laying a deep kiss on his lips. The hand gripping my knee tightened slightly as his whole body relaxed. I broke the kiss a moment later to look up at him.

"Better?" I asked taking my thumb to wipe away the slight red lipstick I had left on his lips.

"Mmhmmm....." Brantley mumbled lowering his head toward mine again. He poked his lip out in a pout when I stopped him with a hand on his chest.

"Later hotshot," I said with a grin. "We are here."

He nodded his head and slid across the seat to the door putting his hand on the handle. He turned back to give me a soft smile.

"I love you Cass," he said picking up my hand to place a quick kiss on my knuckles before opening the door.

"I love you too," I said scooting over so he could help me out. He turned his back to the crowd as he helped me step out before wrapping my arm through his to help me balance on these shoes. Brantley smiled and waved as pictures where snapped. I knew there were probably a few people wondering who was with him.

We made our way down the carpet to take our picture in front of the CMT logo. I had tried to pull away so he could take the photo alone but he banded those leather covered arms around me pulling me closer. We finished posing for pictures and he was waved over to take to a couple of people that were interviewing guests. I recognized Katie Cook from CMT and stopped to let Brantley go ahead as he was handed a microphone. I pulled my phone out of my clutch to snap a quick picture of him as I listened to the conversation.

"BG," Katie said smiling at him. "You've had heck of a run here lately. Nominated for the USA Weekend Breakthrough Artist tonight. Got that acceptance speech planned?"

"No mam," Brantley said laughing and grinning. "I just plan on winging it. It has been a heck of a run. We have been very, very blessed this past year. Been on the road with Eric Church earlier, heading out with Toby Keith now and just found out the other day going to get to a headlining tour this fall. I'm pretty excited about that."

"I bet," Katie said and cut her eyes over at me with a grin. Brantley followed her gaze and stepped over to grab my hand tugging me closer. Shit, this isn't what I wanted attention on tonight. I wanted it to be all about him. "BG, who is this lovely lady that is on your arm this evening?"

A huge grin spread across his face as he looked over to answer her after wrapping an arm around me. "This is my very beautiful girlfriend Cassie Paige. She just got the news a few weeks ago that a pilot she had filmed for the CW has been picked up for a full season," he said giving me a wink. "I'm so damn proud of her."

"B...." I hissed behind my smile pinching his side discreetly.

"I thought you looked familiar Cassie," Katie said grinning at me. "I'm looking forward to the show. How long have y'all been together?"

"A couple of months," Brantley answered. "I actually met her last year. She and my drummer, Ben, are cousins. She came out to a show to see him and knocked my boots off with one look. Took me a while to get her to go out with me but I'm glad she did."

"Well, I can imagine you both stay pretty busy," Katie said. "Who does the most traveling?"

"We both do," I said with a laugh. "A lot of this show will be filmed in Atlanta and I actually live in Athens so I'll be closer to home."

"And you are finishing up your house near Jefferson right BG," Katie said.

"Yes mam," Brantley answered. "Hopefully they will be done with it in the next few months."

"Well," Katie said. "It was good to see you BG as always. Cassie so glad we got to see you. Keep him in line and good luck tonight buddy!"

We made our way to the door hand in hand and Brantley was stopped by Rich walking up to him with grimace on his face as a brunette trailed behind him. I schooled my features when I recognized her.

I had done a couple episodes of One Tree Hill and had been around Jana Kramer a few times. I was not a fan. I took in the short dress, big hair, and heels and all I could think was city girl trying to play country. I watched her eye Brantley up and down as they approached us. Yep, he was hot as hell bitch, but he was all MINE!

"BG," Rich said giving me a half smile. "This is Jana Kramer. She's moving to Nashville and is getting started in the business. Was wanting to know if you would be interested in helping her write a few songs."

"Nice to meet you Miss Kramer," I heard my boyfriend rumble as he politely stuck his hand out to shake her dainty one. I tightened my grip on the belt loops under his jacket. "I don't know what help I would be but I will do what I can."

I smothered a growl underneath a cough and he cut his eyes over at me in amusement. He backed up half a step as she stepped closer to him almost knocking me down and made me want to gag on her cloying perfume. She played with the lapel of his leather jacket giving him a big smile.

"I'm sure you could help me out a lot," she said giving him a flirty smile. I slid my hand into his back pocket looking for the brass knuckles I knew where there. Brantley felt my hand and regained his composure.

"This is my girlfriend Cassie," he said pulling me back close to him making her take a step away.

"Yes," Jana said giving me a fake smile. "We've met before. Nice to see you again Cassie."

"Wish I could say the same Jana," I seethed through clenched teeth as she smirked at me.

"Well," Jana said flipping her hair over her shoulder as she gave Brantley another smile. "Think about it and get back to me. Rich has my number."She turned on a heel and strutted off.

"You better lose that number Rich," I growled pointing at him making him turn pale. I felt myself turned in Brantley's arms as he leaned down closer to my ear.

"Jealous, are we?" he whispered against my ear chuckling.

"Yes," I huffed looking up at him as he smiled down at me picking my hand up to put in the middle of his t-shirt covered chest.

"Baby," he said softly. "That right there is all yours. Hell to be honest, she was kind of scary."

I barked out a laugh as we walked closer to the door. Brantley stopped when he heard someone call his name. I glanced over my shoulder as the couple approached us. I smacked Brantleys arm as my eyes widened.

"B.....B....that's ummm..." I stuttered as he rolled his eyes at me. Ok, maybe I was fangirling a little bit. Brantley stuck his hand out to shake the one the tall brown haired guy with the blonde on his arm held out to him. Good Lord, those teeth were even whiter in person. I was speechless. The pretty blonde I knew to be the man's wife gave me a big smile as Brantley leaned over to give her a big hug.

"Baby," Brantley said pulling me back to his side. "This is Luke and his wife Caroline. Guys, this is Cassie Paige, my girlfriend."

"Girlfriend?" Caroline asked with raised eyebrows as her smile widened. "Been holding out on all of us BG. I thought you knew better."

"Babe," Luke admonished her rolling his eyes. "Leave the poor man alone. Bad enough the torture you put him through a few months back at a bonfire at Jason's. Cassie honey, it is very nice to meet you."

"Ummmum...." I stuttered at a loss for words. Caroline laughed.

"Oh honey," she said squeezing my arm. "Trust me. Luke will make you look at first. Then you quickly realize how big of a goofball, pain in the ass he is."

"Am not," Luke whined narrowing his eyes at her.

"Are too!" Caroline and Brantley both chimed back at him. Rich motioned for the two of us to head in the door.

"Well, that's our cue," Brantley said with a grin. "Good luck tonight Luke."

"Same to you BG," he said threading his fingers with Caroline's. "We'll catch up later at the after party."

Why You Gotta Be So Mean

Brantley's POV

I settled down beside Cassie at the booth we had piled into with Luke and Caroline at one of the after parties. Luke had gone and grabbed a couple shots for them. Cassie had looked at me before taking one to make sure I was good. I had squeezed her knee and nodded my head. Cassie had cracked me up earlier when we had taken our seats during the show.

Woman saw movie stars all the time but she had been having a blast fan-girling over country music stars. Didnt take her long though to start giving Luke as much hell as the rest of us did. I had wanted to introduce her to Jason earlier when we got to the party, but he'd been in the corner arguing with Jessica over something.

I kept my hand on Cassie's bare knee under the table stroking my thumb over it softly moving a little higher each time. Yea, I couldn't resist. She had made me damn near speechless when she walked out in this dress. I took a drink out of my water bottle as I listened to something Luke was telling me and almost choked as I heard what Cassie and Caroline were discussing.

"Ok, since you are gonna be in Atlanta this fall," Caroline said tapping a long nail on the table. "We have got to get together to go dress shopping for the CMA's."

"Sounds like a plan to me," Cassie said with a grin. "I know with that dress, I have got to find something that I will be able to wear something under it. I have been afraid all night I would flash somebody."

"Well you look hot, "Caroline said with a saucy wink. "BG hasn't been able to take his eyes off you all night. But I get it panty lines can be a bitch."

"Yes they can," Cassie said with a laugh as she toasted Caroline.

I leaned over to put my lips against Cassie's ear after moving my hand back down. She leaned against my arm getting closer to me.

"Please, please," I whispered in her ear. "Please tell me that was a joke."

"Ummm...." Cassie answered biting her lip and playing with the straw in her drink. "What are you asking B?"

"Please tell me you were kidding," I said cutting my eyes to her as she wiggled around. "You do have on something under that dress right? Because baby, I only have so much damn willpower and you already test its limits normally."

She shifted to face me better and leaned up to press her lips against my ear making my heart speed up. Lord, if she just only knew what she did to me.

"No joke B," she whispered softly flicking her tongue against my ear. "There is nothing under this dress but smooth, silky, tan skin. Who said you had to control yourself babe? Most certainly was not me."

"I made you a promise baby," I huffed squeezing her knee gently. "Have a little patience with me please."

Cassie pulled her head back to narrow those chocolate brown eyes and glare at me. I was so lost looking in her eyes I didn't notice she had smoothed a soft hand over the front of my jeans until I jerked slightly as she squeezed my dick lightly. I tried to squirm away from her.

"Cassie.....baby, I growled. "Stop."

She kept glaring at me. I could see her cheeks getting redder and I knew she was getting pissed.

"No B," she hisses quietly staring me down. "I won't. Good God, I have been wet since I saw you standing there in that leather jacket. Then you go and turn that damn hat around backwards."

She pointed a finger at me and slid to the edge of the booth standing up. "Fine then. You know what, I'm just gonna get a drink."

I watched shaking my head as she stalked over to the bar the red dress swirling around her as she walked. If that woman just knew how damn beautiful she was. I tamped down a growl as Tyler and BK both almost fell off their stools as Cassie leaned up against the bar. I was serious if Tyler leaned any further over he was going to face plant.

I heard a snicker and turned my head to see Caroline grinning at me.

"Sounds like it may be time to put up or shut up," she said with a giggle.

"Hush Caroline," I growled out tapping my fingers on the table as Luke laughed. I gave her another glare before turning to look back at Cassie. My jaw clenched tightly as I now saw Tyler and BK on either side of the stool she was sitting on chatting away with her.

She turned around to point at me with a smirk and all I could see long tan leg. I glared at her as she waved then turned back to the boys. Pretty sure the damn woman just flashed me on purpose. I heard another laugh and turned my head to see Luke grinning at me as he took a sip of beer.

"Man," he said shaking his head. "If Tyler leans any closer to Cassie, hes gonna fall off that stool."

I watched Cassie laugh at something the boys were telling her as BK hands her a shot. She turned her head slightly to wink at me before tossing it back. I growled deeply as Caroline cracked up laughing at me getting jealous.

"Well BG," Caroline said with a wide grin leaning against Luke's chest. "Are you going to man up and that woman what she so clearly is asking for. Or are you gonna ignore the signals. Didn't take you to be chicken when it comes to giving a girl what she is asking for."

"Caroline," I growled. "You don't understand."

"Well," she said leaning forward to put her arms on the table and glare at me. "Then explain it to me."

"I can't," I muttered getting really interested in looking at my hands.

"Why not?" Caroline scoffed. I sighed as I gave her a look. She looked confused for a minute then her mouth dropped open in shock. "OOOOOhhhh really?"

"Yes," I sighed.

"Does it bother you?" she asked watching my face intently.

"No, not really," I said shrugging my shoulders as I let my gaze wander back over to Cassie. "Little scary, but damn Caroline. I love that woman so damn much. So I am not being a chicken. I just want it to be special for her as she is to me."

"BG," Caroline said reaching a hand across the table to squeeze mine. "You love her. I can tell she loves you and that woman desperately wants you. Stop over thinking it."

"But I don't want it to be something she regrets," I said leaning back in the booth. "I want it to be something that is special as what she is giving to me. She could want anybody, but she wants me."

"Honey close your eyes," Caroline said using her mom voice and out of habit I automatically listened. My own Mama would be proud. "Think about your future. Who do you see by your side with all the things you want to happen? Things you want to do in life."

"Cassie," I answered quietly. I could picture it all so clearly in my head.

"There you go B, "Caroline said softly. "Buddy, when it's that one special person in your life that is your one, it doesn't matter if it is the first or thousandth time you had made love. If that connection is there, it's always going to be special." She studied me closely then smirked. "Been ring shopping online haven't you?"

"What the hell Caroline?" I said in surprise. "Are you psychic now?"

"No not psychic," she said throwing her blonde hair back laughing. "Just can tell you love her and she's your one. Hold onto that honey. Because in this business and hers, it isn't easy. Don't give her reason to doubt how you feel. So saying that, I will say this. She loves you and you are her one. If a woman has waited this long and is telling you that she is ready. Then buddy she is. Believe her and show her with your actions just how precious that gift is. I have a feeling you know how without instruction."

I nodded my head giving her a wink and a smirk that was quickly wiped off my face as Caroline pointed over to the bar. I whipped my head around as a slow song came on and Tyler jumped off his stool to hold a hand out to Cassie.

He helped her step down as he pointed out to the dance floor. I jumped up making Luke laugh and threw my shoulders back slightly. I liked Tyler and all, but dammit that was my woman he was intruding on. I walked over to tap him on the shoulder before he ever could pull Cassie into a dance. BK started laughing so hard as Tyler's eyes widened when he saw me.

I wrapped an arm around Cassie and gave them both a slight nod before I tugged Cassie further out onto the dance floor.

"I think I've got it from here bud," I called out over my shoulder.

"B," Cassie huffed as we stepped to the middle of the floor. "It was just a dance."

"Well baby, "I said lifting her hand to my lips kissing it softly before twining our fingers together and holding them to my chest as I wrapped my other arm around her to sway to the music. "I get the first one."

Out of the corner of my eye I could see and hear Caroline and Luke. She high fived him as he laughed.

"See!" she cheered. "I knew he had skills."

"Woman," Luke said rolling his eyes and kissing her cheek. "I swear if I didn't know that you love me. I would swear you have a thing for the man."

"Nah," Caroline said standing up to pull him out onto the floor. "I just like giving him hell."

"That's the truth," I muttered as they walked by and Cassie giggled against my shoulder.

Cassie's POV

I snuggled my head further into Brantley's chest so he couldn't see the slightly tipsy grin I had on my face. BK and Tyler were right. All it had taken was a little attention from another man and B hopped up real quick to stake his claim. I had been wondering there for a minute. Even discreetly flashed him.

As the song ended Brantley stepped back to pull me off the dance floor behind him. I dug my heels in to yank him back as a good old bump and grind song began to play. I yanked him back closer to me wrapping my arms around his neck giving him a wide grin. I couldn't help but laugh at the shocked expression as I started to swirl my hips to the music.

"Oh come on baby," I said sweetly. "I know you have moves."

He glared down at me before he leaned down to whisper in my ear.

"I've got moves alright," he muttered brushing his lips against my neck sending chills down my spine. "But no one else is going to see them."

"Well," I drawled dragging my nails over the back of his neck making him moan lightly in his throat. "I've only been begging you to show me for a month!"

"Woman, don't you be tempting me," he growled as I pressed my body closer to his. "I have told you my restraint is only so strong."

Well, I thought to myself, let's just see how strong it is. I slid my hand between us to cup him and eased up to whisper into his ear nipping an ear ring between my teeth and tugging.

"What will make that restraint snap?" I whispered huskily. "Hmmmmm?"

He sucked in a deep breath as I moved my hand up and down on his hard on.

"Cassie," he hissed in my ear through clenched teeth.

"Yes baby" I asked innocently batting my eyes at him never moving my hand. I turned in his harms to press my bare back fully against his chest grinding my ass against him along with the beat.

"You need to stop honey," Brantley grumbled in my ear as he wrapped his big body around me.

"No," I said leaning my head back against his shoulder. I felt him grip my hips tightly trying to still them. "I'm gonna make you break."

"No Cass," he stuttered out through gritted teeth as I swiveled my hips. "You..need..to stop."

"Uh uh," I said with a small laugh." I like what I am doing baby. Feels sooooo good."

Brantley pushed me forward gently and stepped back away from me. I whirled around to look up at him glaring. I stepped closer to talk to him so no one could hear us over the music.

"Really B," I hissed poking a finger in his chest. "Really. I put on this sexy ass dress for you. YOU! I bought this with nothing else in mind but wanting to see the look I saw on your face. I wanted to see the desire I saw and see in the eyes of the man that I love. But you keep stepping back. If I couldn't see the evidence proving otherwise.I would think that you didn't want me."

"Oh make no bones about it," Brantley growled crossing his arms to glare at me as he leaned down closer. "I want you. Hell I want you so damn bad my teeth hurt. But it will not be some damn quickie in the bathroom, or hall closet or on the damn tour bus. No darlin, you first time that I make love to you, no that we make love together, will be on a bed with soft sheets. Sheets as soft as your skin. And we will have all the damn time in the world to explore each other and each others bodies. Because I love you and that is what I want for you baby. Its what I want for us."

I blinked back tears as I rubbed my hands on my arms as his words sank in. He wrapped his arms around me pulling me back against his chest.

"Dammit B," I grumbled as I slid my hands under his jacket to clench the back of his shirt. "You don't play fair at all you know that. I was prepared to be pissed off at you the rest of the night. Then you go and say something like that."

"Darlin, I love you," he said dipping his head down to look into my eyes." I think you are hot as hell. And yea, I want to peel that dress off you right now but we have to wait just a little bit longer okay. I promise it wont be long."

I snuggled my head further into his chest and sighed. Another slow song came on and he pulled me tighter to him as we moved to the music.

"I love you too," I said. "I'm trusting you know what you are doing."

He pressed a soft kiss to my forehead before settling his cheek onto the top of my head pulling me closer.

"I do baby," I heard him whisper. "I promise."

17 Again: Part I

July 2012

Cassie's POV

I tossed and turned in my bed trying to get some sleep. A full, bright, summer moon shown through my window. I was tired but couldn't sleep. I wound up not having all the downtime I'd planned on after the awards in June. I was able to get a week before I got the call to head back to L.A. to shoot promos for the new series.

I had been on the road with Brantley at the time. Kelsey had laughed until she cried when I got back in town and she had asked why I was so grouchy. I swear after our argument after the awards, that man had been on a mission. That mission was to drive me crazy!

I turned on my side and punched my pillow trying to get comfortable. Every touch was deliberate. It was like he put a little more into each kiss. Patience my ass. I had done everything I could to push every one of his buttons. If the jackass wasn't going to play fair, then I wasn't either. I had cut off a pair of my jeans to a short enough pair of daisy dukes that Brantley had literally tripped over his feet as I walked by.

Ben had yelled at me to go put some damn clothes on. I had thought for sure I had almost gotten him to cave when he talked me into taking a bike ride with him before I flew out of Denver back to L.A. I'd slid my hands under his t-shirt and kept tracing circles with my nails up and down his abs, to his chest, then back to the top of his jeans.

He'd glared at me so hard when we got back I had flipped him off before stomping back to the bus. His jaw had dropped when he came to climb in bed that night after doing some writing with Jesse and I had taken every pillow I could find to make a barrier between us. If I wasn't getting any, then he wasn't getting any snuggles.

I had flown into Atlanta a couple of hours ago but Brantley wasn't home either. Some bike trip he had already had planned with the boys. Times like this, I could see the downside of our professions and maintaining a relationship. We tried to match our schedules up the best we could. I felt my eyes water a little as I wrapped my arms around the pillow beside me. I was afraid to think about the next year.

If this season went well, I'd be busy filming and I knew he was already writing in preparation of going into the studio next year. I closed my eyes willing myself to get some sleep when I heard something peck against my window making me eyes flew open. I heard it again and sat up quickly in bed listening intently. What the hell was that?

I saw a shadow move near the window and I let out a quiet scream diving for my phone. I automatically hit the speed dial for Brantley even though I knew he was miles away. I heard a small knock on the window as the phone started to ring. Then I could hear a tone right outside the window as I could hear a laugh. I was shaking too bad to even understand.

"Brantley," I hissed glancing towards the window as he answered the phone. "I need help someone is outside my window."

"Baby," he said with a quiet chuckle. "You want to come open this window?"

"Do what?" I snapped throwing the covers back. "That's you! You have a damn key you idiot!"

I stomped over to the window and pull the blinds open to see my boyfriend standing there smirking at me in the moonlight. I narrowed my eyes at him as I hung up the phone then yanked the window up. I crossed my arms glaring at him. He stepped forward brace his arms on the window sill grinning at me. I was trying to stay mad as my heart rate tried to go back to normal.

"Hey beautiful," he said trying to reach for me. I smacked his hand. "What the hell Cass? It was such a beautiful moonlit night I thought I'd try to sneak you out to take a drive. Trying to be romantic."

"Brantley Keith!" I yelled. "You have a damn key. Why not just use it and the front door like a normal person?"

"Baby," he said giving me a smug smirk. Have some will power Cass, I thought. I looked at him standing there with a backwards Bulldogs hat, cut out t-shirt, shorts and grinning at me. "Come on, go throw some shorts on and let's go."

"No," I growled. "You scared the shit out of me."

"I promise it will be worth it," he said pleadingly.

"Fine," I sighed. "Give me five minutes."

I shut the window and hurried over to my dresser pulling out a pair of shorts to wear with his Led Zeppelin t-shirt I had stolen a while back. I slipped a pair of flip flops on then grabbed my phone. I walked out the house after locking it to look up and see him standing leaned up against his truck.

"Alright hotshot," I asked walking over to him. "Where to?"

"Well," Brantley said with a smirk and opening his door so I could climb in the middle. "Your chariot awaits madam."

He hopped in after me and started his truck, but stopped to turn and look at me instead of backing out of my driveway. He crooked his finger at me to lean closer. I did and felt my heart beat faster as he moved closer to place a long, slow, kiss on my lips. I fisted my hands into his shirt tugging him closer. He laughed against my lips as he pulled away.

"Mmm," he said kissing my cheek and placing a hand on my leg. "Think it is safe to say you missed me. Even if you were aggravated with me before you left."

"Had good reason to be," I grumbled under my breath as he pulled off my street and onto the highway. The radio was playing quietly in the background. "Damn tease."

"You weren't playing fair either baby," he laughed turning on the road to head towards Jefferson. "Those damn shorts almost killed me. Then that shit on the bike."

"Well," I said cutting my eyes over at him and smiling. "Do you blame me?"

"No darlin," Brantley said shaking his head. "Not at all."

He wrapped an arm around my shoulders pulling me into his side as he drove. I relaxed into his side with a sigh as he pressed a soft kiss to my temple. I didn't need fancy dinner dates or red-carpet premieres like most women in my line of work. Give me a moonlit night and some country backroads any day.

17 Again: Part II

Brantley's POV

I glanced down at Cassie as I drove. She had fallen asleep with her head on my shoulder about fifteen minutes outside of Athens. I smiled and slowed down to turn into the driveway of my house. They still had some things to finish up. But the part I had been pushing to be done was completed. I eased down the driveway and parked in front of the house smiling at it being illuminated by the moonlight. I had left a few lights on earlier before I had left to head to Cassie's.

I put the truck in park, killing the engine, the looked over at Cass still sound asleep. I chuckled to myself as I eased the door open to step out then tugged her over lifting her into my arms to make my way into the house. I walked into the front door feeling her sigh against my neck as I eased the door shut.

Woman could sleep anywhere most of the time. I had noticed the faint circles under her eyes when she opened the window but would do me no good to say anything. Cassie would go wide open as long as she could. I couldnt argue. I was the same damn way. Maybe I could persuade her to rest over the next couple of days. I carefully made my way up the stairs to the finished part of the house and down the hall to what would be my room.

We'd been so busy and at home at different times, I hadn't brought Cassie out here to show her. Kolby and I had spent all day lugging the massive king-sized bed I had bought up here and getting it set up. I had thought of tons of ideas on what to do but always circled back to the same one.

I always came back to the idea of being able to make love to her the first time in the house I hoped one day we would both call home. I laid Cassie down gently on the bed, then kicked off my shoes before tossing my and hat and shirt to join them. I slipped her flip flops off as she settled down on the pillow in the middle stirring slightly.

"B," she murmured blinking her eyes open as I stretched out beside her pulling her closer.

"Yes baby?" I said leaning over to place a soft slow kiss on her lips. I stifled a moan as she smiled sleepily and pushed her body against mine trying to get closer.

"Where are we?" she asked burying her head into my neck as I felt her yawn.

"The house," I said softly as I wrapped my arms around Cassie tighter and rolled to my back taking her with me. She stretched out on top of me wiggling a little to get comfortable. She lifted her head resting her chin on my chest and looked up at me. She half smiled and arched an eyebrow at me.

"You mean to tell me that you drug me out of my perfectly comfortable bed to drive me to another one," Cassie giving me a look as I tugged her up closer and ran my hands up and down her back. I couldn't help but chuckle as she moved her leg over the sheets slightly. "But damn if it isn't soft."

"Yes, baby doll," I said with a grin running a hand through her hair pulling her face down to mine. "I did."

I kissed her deeply banding my arms around her waist then rolling her over to her back as she moaned deep in her throat as I settled between her legs. I bit her lip making her gasp sliding my tongue between her soft lips to tangle mine with hers. Cass sank her nails into my bare shoulders making me shift to get closer to her.

"B," she growled pushing both hands into my chest to glare up at me. "You have gotta stop teasing me. Its past the point of being unfair."

I smirked and leaned down to trail kisses from her shoulder where my shirt had slipped, up her neck, to her ear nipping the lobe gently.

"Who says I'm teasing?" I murmured rocking my hips forward to brush my erection against her. Cass whimpered in the back of her throat then narrowed her eyes at me.

"Because," she muttered under her breath. "That's exactly what you have been doing for the last two months."

I raised my head and glided both hands under her back pulling her up slightly to hover my lips an inch away from hers. I could feel her heart pounding against my chest.

"I promised you special," I whispered sweeping my lips against hers softly. I chuckled against her lips at the growl I heard escape. I could see her glaring at me.

"Dammit B," she whined pulling her head back. "I am about ready to explode and you keep this up."

"Baby girl," I said quietly lifting a hand to point around the moon lit room. I knew Cassie well enough that she didnt need the flowers, soft music, or

candlelight. I knew all she wanted was us. "This is what I was waiting on.
I pushed to get this part of the house finished. Because when I thought
about making love to you the first time, all I could think was that I wanted
it to be in this house. The one I hope and pray we both call home one day."

My heart sped up as I watched the tears well up in Cassies eyes. Shit,
please tell me I didn't upset her. The thought crossed my mind half a
second before she grabbed my chin yanking my head down kissing me hard
molding her body to mine. She broke the kiss a second later and smiled up
at me.

"Then I suggest you better make love to me hotshot," she growled wrapping her legs around me. I could feel how hot she was through her shorts.
"Show me everything B, because I feel like I am on fire."

I smirked down at her and shifted my weight against her pushing her
further into the mattress rocking against her.

"Oh baby," I said with a dark grin. "You haven't seen anything yet. There is
one problem though Cass." I gripped the edge of my shirt leaning back to
tug it over her head. "You're wearing too many clothes."

Cassie give me a sexy smile. "We both are," she murmured trailing her hands
down my chest to the top of my shorts then sliding her hands across the top
of my ass pushing them down. She stopped after a second and just stared.
Then looked back up at me blinking before looking down again. Cass
eased a soft hand between us to circle the shaft of my hard cock squeezing
slightly.

A sound between a growl and a moan escaped out of my throat as I closed
my eyes against the feeling.

"Woman," I muttered as I placed my hand on top of hers to stop her.
"Unless you want me to cum like I am sixteen again, you better be careful."

I leaned down to capture a hard pink nipple between my teeth making Cassie moan and arch closer to me. I let the nipple go with a wet pop making her gasp as I tugged the edge of her shorts down. I looked down at her and a wide grin spread across my lips as I looked back up at her. I could see a faint blush over her skin in the moonlight.

"Hmm.. noootttthhhhhiiinnnn darling?" I asked with a chuckle. She smirked and shrugged a tan shoulder at me.

"Well, you did wake me up," she said as I slid her shorts the rest of the way off and settled back against her. "Be lucky I even had your shirt on."

I pressed my body closer to hers making her moan quietly. Feeling unsure of myself, I leaned down bracing my arms on either side of Cassies head and took a hand to smooth the hair away from her face. I looked deep into her chocolate brown eyes with question.

"Baby," I asked softly. "Are you sure?"

"B," she growled wrapping her arms around my neck tugging my lips down to hers. "I've never been more sure of anything in my life."

"Well then," I whispered against her lips shifting my hips up to brush against her wet folds making her whimper. "Better hang on to something.
'

Cassie let out a gasp at my words as I ghosted my hand down her body and pressed her hard nub with my thumb.

Sweet Jesus B, Cassie hissed shifting against the sensation as I circled her clit with my thumb. "What are you doing to me?"

"I'm about to show you just what your body can do," I said chuckling darkly nipping her neck and sliding a finger into her wet heat. "So, hold on tight baby doll."

Cassie sank her nails into my shoulders as I stilled my finger letting her get used to the sensation before sliding it in and out and adding a second finger to the first still stroking her clit with my thumb. She let out a low moan right before she stopped breathing causing me to stop.

"Cass, baby?" I asked looking down at her in question. Her eyes were squeezed shut. A low growl was my answer.

"B.... if you stop one more damn time," she grumbled sucking in a deep breath.

"Baby doll," I said with a grin as she cracked an eye open to glare at me. "You've got to breath. You stop, I stop. Understand. Plus, this is gonna take a while. May wanna relax."

"I'm trying to relax you ass," she muttered as I let out a chuckle and shifted my body so I could slide further down hers as I resumed my assault. "But I'm so damn on edge its not even funny. All you have done is tease me!"

She was cut off when I settled between her thighs and leaned forward to replace my thumb with my long tongue with a hard flick to her clit. Cassie let out a sound that was a cross between a yelp and a moan as I did it again. "Shit...."

She threw her head back arching her hips to get closer as I licked, nibbled and lapped all around her throbbing clit never stopping the movement of my fingers in her wet pussy. I kept up the pace and knew she was getting close. I could feel her nails dig deeper into my shoulders and her legs wrap tighter around them. I nipped her clit gently and felt her soaking pussy tighten around my fingers.

"Cum for me baby," I murmured nipping her again making her whimper as I curled my fingers inside her. "Cum for me right now."

Cassie went over the edge with a cry digging her nails in and squeezing me with her thighs. Her whole body arched off the bed and I could see her toes curl from the corner of my eye. I gently eased my fingers out of her lapping her pussy one more time making her shudder as I kissed my way back up her body to her neck. Her chest was heaving against mine.

"You ok there baby?" I asked huskily as a chocolate brown eye cracked open to look up at me as a giddy smile broke out across her face.

"I am. But I need more. I know you've got more than that in you, "she murmured putting her hands on my chest and running them down to my V line and circling my hard cock with one soft hand. Her eyes widened when she realized her fingers didn't meet. I shifted forward in her hand and leaned down to kiss her deeply plunging my tongue in her mouth to flick against hers giving her a taste of herself.

"Oh," I said pulling back to nibble on her full bottom lip. "I've got plenty more darlin."

"Yea," Cassie snarked with a grin. Always my favorite little smart ass. "I can feel. But how the hell is this gonna work Brantley."

"Slowly," I murmured against her lips as I pushed forward against her feeling her suck in a deep breath as my hard cock slid between her wet lips. I paused to grit my teeth against the warmth and wetness and noticed Cassie wince slightly as I stretched her. "Eyes baby. Let me see those eyes. Never take them off mine ok. That way I know I am not hurting you anymore than I have to." I kissed her against never breaking eye contact as I pulled my hips back eased forward again. I stilled when I met up with resistance and pulled back to slide in slowly again.

"Baby," Cassie moaned lifting her hips up making me sink further. "Just do it. Please..... Make me yours in every way possible."

What little bit of control I had let snapped as I pushed further into her breaking the barrier and my heart almost broke at the sheen of tears in her eyes. I stilled after burying to the hilt in her. I opened my mouth to ask if she was ok when glared at me before I could. "I'm fine B. I promise. But you have got to move dammit. Please....."

I lifted my hands up to ease hers off my shoulders linking our fingers together shifting them over her head and pressing my body tighter to hers as I started to move. Cassie let out a whimper as she moved her hips along with mine increasing the rhythm. I used over joined hands as leverage to lift up slightly to look down at her.

Cassie's eyes were rolled back into her head as I increased my thrusts making her tighten around me. She wrapped her legs around my hips pulling me closer to her. I knew she was close again just from the look in her eyes. I swiveled my hips around as I bucked up hard. Cassie screamed as she went over the edge with a gasp and tightened around my dick milking me and triggering my own orgasm.

"Fuck," I muttered as I buried my face in her neck and tried to regain my senses. Heaven help me, if she had felt this damn good just the first time, I was in trouble. I unlocked my fingers from hers and raised my head to look into her eyes as I smoothed the dark hair away from her face. "Baby, you ok?"

Cassie blinked trying to focus tightening her hold on me. The slight movement earned a moan from me as my dick slid back into her again.

"Mmmm...." she mumbled giving me a half sleepy grin. "Oh baby, I am more than ok. I can see why I need to toss my damn toys away now. Consider them trashed!!"

I couldn't help it I started to chuckle as she yawned and that grin widened.

"I just bet you are," I said quietly as I slipped out of her making her whimper and rolled to my side taking her with me. I banded my arms around her as she snuggled into my side placing a soft kiss on my chest. I lifted a hand to tug the covers over us as my eyes started to get heavy.

"I love you," Cassie murmured holding me closer to her. "I'm so glad that I waited for you."

"Love you too baby," I whispered slipping a finger under her chin lifting her lips to mine. "I don't think I have the words to explain how humbled I am. I know without a doubt, you were made for me. Get some rest. I can promise round two later. I've gotten just a taste and I want more."

Baking and Tree Decorating

D ecember 18, 2012

Cassie's POV

"B," I said with a laugh smacking his hand away from the bowl of cookie dough I was mixing to finish the Christmas cookies I had been working on. Brantley had both arms wrapped around my waist in the kitchen at his house. He had moved in a couple months ago and I had been spending as much time here as I could when I had time off. He was trying his damnedest to snag a bite and I wasn't having it. He drug his beard along my neck making me laugh harder. "You've got to stop."

"Nope," he murmured pushing me into the counter with his hips grinning. "I've got ya right where I want you baby."

"And at this rate I will never get the cookies I promised your Mama I would bake done," I said pushing back against him making him moan and spin me around. He picked me up to sit me on the granite counter with a grin. He reached up to brush a stray lock of hair off my face then rubbed a smudge of flour off my cheek. "You get the dang tree put up mister?"

"Yes mam," he murmured burying his face into my neck kissing his way up to my ear and biting it gently. "All done and just waiting on you to get done in here to put the ornaments on."

"Give me just a little bit and I will be finished," I said tracing my nails on the back of his neck trying to unwrap my legs from his waist, but he wasn't having it.

"Or....." Brantley drawled pulling his head back giving me a mischievous grin. "We can put off doing the tree. Break in these counter tops.'

"We've already done that," I murmured leaning over to kiss his lips. "Twice."

"Oh yea," he said pulling his head back tapping his chin. "Surely there is somewhere in this house we have left to christen, right?"

"I think we have thoroughly covered our bases," I said with a giggle and kissed his cheek pushing him back. I swiped my finger in the sugar cookie dough holding it out to him with a smile. Brantley grabbed my wrist and eased my finger up to his mouth sucking it in with a smile. I bit the inside of my cheek to keep a whimper in. He let my finger go with a pop and smirked down at me.

"Baby," he said with a grin. "Why don't you put those in the fricge and I'll help you with them after we decorate the tree?"

"Fine," I said rolling my eyes then pointing a finger at him. "But you're not eating all the dough mister."

"Yes mam," he drawled with a wink backing up to help me down. "Scouts honor."

"Boy scout my ass," I said with a snort and covered the bowl of dough up to put away. I jumped letting out a yelp when I felt sharp smack to my ass. These black yoga pants I had on with one of his sweatshirts did little to protect me from his big hands. "Ow B. Stop harassing me and go light the fire please."

He strolled out of the kitchen with a laugh shaking his sweat pant covered ass at me. He had been home about a week and I had wrapped filming until after the first of the year the other day. We had gone earlier after we had finally dragged ourselves out of bed to get a tree and decorations. I was glad we both had some down time together.

I paused after putting the dough up to brace my hands on the cool counter top biting my lip. I was already worried with how busy we were both going to be this upcoming year. I shook it off with a sigh then headed towards the living room. I let out a gasp as I walked in.

The huge tree we had picked out was covered in soft twinkling white lights that cast a soft glow around the room along with the fire Brantley had gotten going. It had just gotten dark so they were the only light in the room. I was glad we were having a bit of a cold spell so we could enjoy it.

"Babe," I said with a grin walking over to the tree to run my fingers over the branches. I hadn't really done much for Christmas since my parents had passed away. I was looking forward to this one though. "It looks beautiful."

"Not nearly as beautiful as you," he said walking over to join me looking just as comfortable as me in his sweatpants and t-shirt. Brantley pressed a soft kiss to my lips then handed me a box of the ornaments we had chosen. "Here, you take low and I'll take high."

We both worked quickly placing the ornaments on the tree. I could hear him humming lowly and he'd glance over to give me a smile every once in a while. He had been writing a good bit for the next album but wouldn't let me hear any of it. The ass. I placed my last ornament on the tree and let out a squeak of surprise when Brantley gripped my hips leaning down. He put me on his shoulders then picked the angel tree topper up off the nearby couch handing it to me to put on. I got her situated then plugged her in.

"Ok," I said kissing the top of his head. "Let me down. I want to see how she looks."

He sat me down on my feet then tugged me into his arms as we stepped back slightly to look at our handy work. I leaned back further into his chest with a sigh and smiled when I felt a light kiss on my cheek.

"Turned out great," he said pulling me closer. I don't think I would ever get enough of this man. He snapped his fingers together making me jump and dropped his arm. "Shit. We forgot one. Mama got this made for us."

He walked over to the table by his recliner to pick up a white box. He stepped back over to me and placed it in my hands. I opened the lid and gasped as I pulled out a beautiful round silver Christmas ball with the year 2012 scripted on it in black with both of our signatures on it.

Now I knew why Mama Becky had wanted me to sign something after Thanksgiving. Brantley handed me a hook for it with a soft smile. I slipped it through the black and silver ribbon before moving closer to the tree. As I went to hang it, I noticed the slight rattle from it.

"B," I said worriedly cutting my eyes around to him. He was standing there with his arms crossed watching me intently. "It's rattling. I didn't break it did I?"

"Don't think so baby," he answered shrugging his shoulders nonchalantly. "But check it to make sure."

I nodded my head then studied the ornament. My eyes narrowed as I realized it could be opened. Knowing my luck, Kolby stuck something in there to mess with me. I used my thumbs to open it gently with one eye closed in fear at what I would find.

However, what I did find had me covering my mouth with one hand in shock. I felt heat against my back as Brantley stepped behind me wrapping an arm around my waist and reaching for the ornament with the other as I started to cry.

"Is that real?" I whispered. I felt his chest rumble with a quiet laugh as he turned me around to face him. I was quickly wiping the tears from my eyes but the effort was wasted when he slowly sank to a knee on the hardwood floor smiling up at me.

"Yes mam," he said with a quick wink holding the beautiful diamond ring in his fingers. I could see his hands shaking slightly as he reached for mine. "It is very real. Cassandra Nicole Paige, I love you more than I can tell you some days. You complete and settle me in ways I never dreamed of finding. I couldnt my blessings every day for you being brought into my life and to me there was no better way to celebrate my one year of sobriety than this. So, will you do me the honor of being my wife? I want to be able to spend the rest of my life loving you."

"Yes," I choked out between tears as he slid the ring of my finger and let out a big breath like he had been holding it. Brantley jumped to his feet slamming his lips down on mine kissing me so deeply my head felt like it was spinning. I gripped his shoulders to keep my knees from buckling. He pulled back with a broad grin then picked me up to spin me around the room with a laugh. I wrapped my arms and legs around his waist holding on. He stopped then looked at me pushing the hair away from my face.

"Are you sure?" he said giving me a sly grin. "I know I'm a catch and all but I mean, if you are gonna back out now is the time." He growled at me when I cuffed the side of his head.

"Oh, shut up ass," I said sticking my tongue out at him making him smirk. "Of course, I'm sure."

"Good," he murmured darkly leaning his lips down to mine and walking us towards the rug in front of the fireplace. "Because you're not getting rid of me baby."

He lowered me to the floor then stretched out beside me as I tugged the end of his beard pulling him closer.

"I love you beautiful," he whispered kissing me softly as I wrapped my arms around his neck. "Thank you for making me the happiest man in the world."

"I love you hotshot," I said with a wink biting his lip. "There's nowhere else I would rather me."

2013: What A Wonderful Year

B rantley's POV

I walked out of the kitchen from putting up dishes on Christmas Day and saw Cassie leaned against the doorway watching everyone. I had told Mama that Cassie and I both wanted to have it here this year. I know it if wasn't for this, we both would be exactly where we had been the last few days and that was in bed. We both had made the mistake of looking at our calendars the other day trying to decide on a wedding date.

At this point I couldn't tell you who would be out of town more, me or her. I had done everything I could to assure Cassie that we could make this work, no problem. We loved each other, that was all we needed. If a wedding didn't get planned this year, there was always next year. Just as long as I got to call her my wife. I knew it was hard on her not having her parents here. So far Ben was the only one who knew I had proposed to her because I had asked his permission

. He had been floored at first when I brought up the subject. But I had assured him that while it may seem fast, I couldnt imagine not spending the rest of my life with her. I eased behind her wrapping my arms around her waist and settled my chin into the crook of her neck kissing her sweater covered shoulder softly.

"You okay baby?" I asked quietly as she leaned back against my chest.

"Yea," she whispered back turning to kiss me softly. "I'm fine B. I promise."

"Awww... look Becky," Shelia, Ben's mom said with a laugh from the couch. "Look who is standing under the mistletoe." Cassie and both looked at each other then up and grinned. I could hear my mama laugh along with her as I turned Cass around to face me leaning down to her.

"Oh, come on!" Ben yelled as Kolby groaned. "Don't give them another excuse to make out please! We see enough of this on the road."

I flipped him off over Cassie's shoulder as I slid my hand down to palm her ass just to make Ben squirm as I kissed her deeply making her whimper quietly.

"Keep that up mister," Cassie mumbled against my lips a moment later. "And you will find yourself flat on your back in that big bed up there."

"I have created a monster let me tell you," I said with a chuckle kissing her cheek. "You ready to tell everyone?"

"Yea," she whispered with a smile. I pulled her ring out of my pocket where she had slipped it earlier when everyone started showing up and slid it back on her finger where it would stay from now on.

June 2013

Brantley's POV

"Cassandra Nicole," I growled lowly into the phone as I paced. I kept looking up at the arrival board at the airport. "Your plane landed twenty minutes ago. Just where the fuck are you!"

I heard the beep signaling the end of the voice mail and pulled the phone away. Out of the corner of my eye I saw the flash of a photographer. Just fucking great I thought as I saw the wet behind the ears reporter making his way over to me. I was thankful I had my dark glasses on to hide the murder in my eyes. I had gotten into Nashville last night and Cass was supposed to fly in this morning to meet me for the CMT awards tonight. The little shit smirked at me as he approached. PJ stepped in front of me with crossed arms.

"Little lady stand you up BG?" the punk said with a smirk. "Or has she moved on?"

"What the fuck did you just say to me?" I growled bowing my arms up. He kept grinning and pulled his phone out to show me. Apparently, the latest headline was that new Hollywood It Girl, Cassie Paige, had been photographed earlier not wearing a ring on a very important finger.

My jaw clenched in anger as the guy watched me for a reaction. This was big news after the last go around a few weeks ago of pictures flying around of her and her co-star and onscreen love interest at dinner together in Atlanta. I had been in New York at the time.

"Come on BG," he said shrugging his shoulders. "Give us some kind of statement. The two of you haven't even been seen together since the ACM's in April. Y'all announced your engagement in January. Shouldn't we all have a date by now?"

"Why you little..." I growled cracking my knuckles making him pale and take a step back. PJ stopped me with a hand on my arm.

"Not here Boss," he said lowly in my ear and gripped my arm turning me around. "Let's go."

I turned on a booted heel typing out an angry text message to my fiancée as I stopped out to the truck. PJ climbed in to drive not trusting my judgement right now. I stopped typing as my phone rang in my hand. I saw it was Cassie and stabbed the answer button.

"Want to explain to me what the fuck is going on?" I growled through clenched teeth. PJ shook his head at me for the tone of voice I was taking with her, but I didn't care right now. She promised me she would be here, and she wasn't.

I could hear all kinds of noise in the background. The best I could remember she wasn't filming anything right now.

"B," she sighed then put her hand over the phone to muffle answering a question. "Look I told you last week I wasn't going to be able to be there. This photo shoot came up. I couldn't get out of it."

"Are you fucking kidding me Cass!" I yelled losing my temper. This was a recurring theme nowadays. Nothing and I mean nothing seemed to be able to be rescheduled. "You didn't tell me a damn thing!"

"Yes, I did!" she snapped back. "I told you on the phone before your show in Phoenix, plus I emailed you and Rich both."

"I don't know what you are talking about," I grumbled digging in my pocket for my cigarettes. PJ cut his eyes at me then mouthed "yes you do". I rolled my eyes and flipped him off. "Or at least I don't remember you telling me honey. I had a song stuck in my head I was trying to get down."

"Look B," Cassie said. I could see her shaking her head from here. "I've got to go. I'm sorry again ok. We'll talk later ok."

"Damn right we will," I grumbled pinching the bridge of my nose. "I'll be home in two days Cass. Expect to fucking talk then."

I hung up the phone and tossed it into the cup holder.

"Little tough on her you think Boss?" PJ said never taking his eyes off the road.

"Don't even start with me," I snarled. "She knew this was important to me."

"And like you haven't cancelled or missed a half a dozen things important to her lately," PJ said matter of factly. "That interview for Country Music Weekly could have been pushed. Rich even offered to push it back a few days, so you could have kept your plans to go see her. But you didn't. Y'all both are in high demand and spread thin. How you going to make a marriage work like that BG?"

"I don't know," I muttered turning to look out the window shutting the conversation down.

Two days later I turned into Cassie's driveway just a little after dark. I hadn't been able to leave the studio in Nashville as early as I had planned. She hadn't returned any of my calls in the last couple of days, but I knew she was home. She had called Mama to let her know she had landed and made it back. Same thing that I always did.

Mama had tried to question me on what was going on. I would almost swear she muttered "stubborn jackasses" under her breath because she didn't get a straight answer out of me either. I leaned my head back against the driver's seat of my truck and stared at Cassies front door. Hell, we'd been engaged for six months and I could literally count on both hands the nights we had actually slept in the same bed since. I'd tried to get her to move her stuff out to the house but she'd firmly refused. Gritting my teeth, I opened my truck door then slammed it behind me as I stalked to the house.

Cassie's POV

I kept blinking to keep my eyes open. Just a little more unpacking then you can crash Cass, just a little more. The makeup artist from the photo shoot for the cast had complained about the circles under my eyes and I had just snarled at her. My agent had tried to calm me down, but I warned her that if she booked me anything else for the next couple of weeks I just may shoot her.

The show had been a hit and we were all in high demand. This also brought a constant watch on my relationship with country music's hottest bad boy as well. I missed Brantley so much it physically hurt right now. I had been purposely avoiding his calls the last couple of days just because I didn't have the energy to fight with him. I know he was hurt I missed the awards.

But I had told him I wasn't going to be able to make it. He'd only been half listening because they had been in the middle of a song writing session when I had called. I pulled my makeup bag out of my suitcase then trudged to bathroom to put it up. I stilled, and my head jerked up when I heard a door slam. I braced my hands on the counter when I heard keys followed by heavy footsteps. I bit my lip and tamped down a tired moan when I heard my name bellowed. I didn't have the energy to argue with him right now. I really didn't.

"CASSIE!" Brantley yelled. I could hear his footsteps getting closer so I walked out of the bathroom into my bedroom. I stopped with crossed arms meeting his glare head on as he walked in. He paused with hands on his hips glaring at me.

" There a problem with your phone? Because you sure as fuck haven't answered it the last few days."

"I've been busy B," I grumbled pointing at him. "That and I really am not in the mood to fight with you right now."

"Well tough shit sweetheart," he snarled. "I've got questions and I am gonna get some answers. Can't hang up or not answer the phone on me now. I want to fucking know why in the hell you were photographed not wearing your ring? Then you stand me up! Am I not worthy of your precious time now Miss Thing!"

I stalked forward and pushed his broad chest hard making him stumble back in surprise. I had been pissed off at him for two weeks and just hadn't been able to say anything. Well, if he wanted to fight, he had one on his hands. "I had fucking taken it off because I was in the middle of filming a retake," I snarled. "I had run out to grab a coffee because I was dead in my feet needed a pick me up. It was on the chain around my neck, where it always goes Brantley. You, know this!"

"Well, thats not how it looked," he grumbled leaning against the wall crossing his arms to look at me. I paced around my own temper getting wound up.

"Really Mr. Country BadAss! I told you two weeks ago they rescheduled that photo shoot for the show," I said angrily pulling stuff out of my suitcase to give me something to do. I needed something to focus on before I started tossing things at his head. "I told you I wouldn't be able to make the awards. If I had to choose to miss one of them I'd rather it have been those! But you've had your head so buried in new music and that studio I doubt you even remember that I told you!"

"You didn't tell me that Cass!" he yelled throwing his hands up. "I get fucking blindsided at the damn airport, by fucking TMZ mind you, with pictures and headlines of you not wearing your ring. I looked like a damn idiot pacing and waiting on my fiancée to land but you never showed. And while we are on the subject, want to explain the photos from the week before last of you out to dinner with your damn costar! Looked pretty cozy with Josh to me!"

"It wasn't just us Brantley!" I yelled shouldering past him to stalk down the hall to the kitchen. I needed a drink. He was hot on my heels. I pulled the bottle of red wine I had in the cabinet down only to have it snatched out of my hand and pushed out of the way. He grabbed my arm to spin me around to look at him. I could see the hurt, anger, and frustration in his green eyes. I knew they were mirrored in my own. Well, join the club mister. I poked a finger into his chest making him growl.

"We just happened to be the last ones at the table. You want to accuse me of shit! Well then. Explain to me why I had to find out from Jessa, Ben's ex, that you saw Amber a couple of weeks ago when you were home. Couldn't tell me that huh! As far as the awards, I told you. I emailed you and Rich both copies of my updated schedule!"

"I don't remember seeing it," he grumbled picking me up to sit on the counter. He tried to reach for me but I stopped him with a raised hand. I was so tired I felt all the fight go out of me. I buried fingers in my hair in frustration as the tears welled up. We remained quiet for a few moments. Our harsh breathing the only sounds in the quiet house.

"Jesus B," I whispered. "I can't keep doing this. I can literally count on one hand. ONE! How many times we have actually seen each other in the last four months? We are supposed to be building a life together and here we stand accusing each other of things?"

"Cass, I'm sorry," he said bending to look into my lowered eyes. "I didn't tell you about Amber. There was nothing to tell. She had asked to see me. We talked nothing more baby. Said she was happy that I had found someone, gotten my life together, and was living my dream. Nothing more."

He stepped in between my legs wrapping his arms around me. I lost the last shred of control I had and started sobbing as I buried my head into the soft black t-shirt he was wearing. I missed him so much when we were apart. I literally couldn't sleep worth a damn some nights if I wasnt wrapped up in his arms. He let out a shaky breath and kissed the top of my head holding me tighter.Like he was afraid I was going somewhere.

"I know baby. I know that even as much as I love you, I can't keep doing this either. It kills me not being able to see you. We have to rely on our managers to schedule our time together. You're right, how can we make a marriage work if we don't see each other."

"Even as much as we want this," I mumbled pulling my head back and I died a little at the sheen of tears in his eyes. "Things arent gonna change, are they?" I wiped at the tears on my face and bit my lip. "Neither of us is going to give up anything right now. We've "supposedly" been planning a wedding. But I've hardly had time to even think about what I'd want let alone talk to you about it."

I pushed him away from me making him step back. I hopped down and braced my hands on the island in the middle of the kitchen. I traced a finger over the well-worn wood as the memories of baking all kinds of things with my mom floated through my mind. How my Dad always could find her here and would wrap his arms around her.

I wanted memories like that. I thought we had started those but then our demanding careers had gotten in the way. To be this miserable wasn't fair to either of us. I turned slightly and met Brantleys eyes as the tears fell harder. I lifted my hand to reach for my ring. His eyes widened with horror and he put a hand out to stop me.

"No Cass," he said shaking his head vehemently. "That is not what I want. I know it can't be what you want either. Baby, please, please, don't."

"Then tell me some other way B," I sobbed wrapping my arms around myself and dodging him when he tried to reach for me. I walked around to put the island between us. At this point it might as well been an ocean.

"I don't see one. We aren't even making the effort to make this relationship work. So how could we even begin to make a marriage work!"

"Baby, you are killing me," he whispered walking around to me. He stopped in front of me staring down with tears in his eyes. "Please, please, don't take it off. We'll figure something out. Ok. Cassie, I'm begging I will do anything. Anything. I'll cut back....."

I stopped him with a gentle finger on his lips and wiped a tear away with the back of my hand. I was trying to keep my own at bay but having no luck.

"That's just it hotshot," I said putting a hand on his chest over his heart. He brought his up to squeeze mine. The cool metal of his rings sent a shiver down my spine at the memory of them on my heated skin when we made love. "We are both locked into so many commitments right now, neither of us can cut anything out. What if it never changes?"

He heaved out a hefty sigh pulling his cap off and sitting it down. He took both hands running them over his head and face in frustration and groaned. "I don't know Cass. All I know is that I love you. I thought that was supposed to be the hardest part you know. Finding the one who you love beyond anything. But turns out, that's been the easy part with us. The hard part is finding the time to see each other in person. Hell lately, its been finding the time to have a five-minute conversation."

"And I love you," I sobbed out the ache in my chest so bad I could barely breath. "So damn much. But B, I can't give you what you want right now or need. You need someone by your side. A family. You need what Luke and Caroline have and I'm not able to give you that right now. The ache in your voice when we are hundreds of miles apart kills me a little more each time we talk. I've been failing you."

Brantley stepped closer cupping my face in both big hands brushing away tears as they fell. He looked at his feet before looking back up at me.

"And I have been failing you Cass," he murmured. "Every time that I have had to cancel dinner plans or a date because of an interview, I can see the disappointment in your eyes or hear it in your voice. Even though you try to hide it from me. Yes. I do want what Luke and Caroline have. I want a family. But Cassie, I want a family with you. Not anyone else. Just you."

"And I can't give you that," I whisper quietly. "Not right now I can't."

"Then when?" he asks softly. I felt his body go rigid because we both knew the answer before it ever left my lips.

"That's just it," I choked out. "I don't know. Maybe..maybe its better this way."

I looked down at my hands and the twinkling ring there one more time then let out a shaky breath as I slipped the ring out my finger. I instantly missed the weight and the feel of it there. I sniffled as I looked up then reached for Brantley's hand to put it in his palm. He backed up shaking his head at me glaring.

"No," he murmured not looking at me. "That is your ring. We may be saying we arent getting married, but I can promise. I am not giving up on us."

I tried to step closer and he kept backing away from me. "B, please don't make this any harder than it already is," I sobbed.

"No," he growled stalking closer and tugging me to him. "I mean it Cassie. I am not giving up. I love you too damn much."

"B, please don't do this," I begged clinging to him. "Please don't. I don't know how long it will be before things could even change."

He pulled me tighter to him and buried his face in my neck as I felt his shoulders heave. I lost track of how long we both stood there holding each other. How was I even going to do this? I just knew we couldn't keep going like we were. We would eventually hate each other.

"Then," he murmured in my ear kissing my cheek. "I'll wait." He slid a hand under my chin to make me look at him. "I'm not giving you up. I love you too damn much to even be able to." I felt his rough hand slide underneath the collar of his t-shirt I was wearing pulling out the chain I had gotten to wear.

Anytime I took my ring off for filming, it went around my neck. Wardrobe knew by now that if the outfit for the scene showed it, then it was time to find something else. I would not take it off. If I couldn't have it on my finger, it would be right next to my heart. The current heart that was breaking into a million pieces.

Brantley gently undid the clasp and then picked my ring up out of my palm before sliding it onto the chain and redoing the clasp. He swallowed roughly and cleared his throat as he blinked back tears. "Keep it safe. Even if it's just so you dont forget me."

He brushed a soft kiss across my lips before backing away and turning on his heel to walk out. I heard the front door close then the slamming of his truck door.

My knees gave out then as I started to sob so hard I could barely breath. Did that really just happen? Had I really just broken the heart of the only man I had and ever will love? I wasn't sure how long I was curled up on the cold kitchen tiles crying when a thought crossed my mind. I sat up abruptly and ran into my room for my phone. With shaky hands I scrolled through my contacts and pushed the number. It rang a couple of times then they answered.

"Hey sweetheart," Kolby boomed with a big laugh. "How's my soon to be sister in law doing?"

"Kolbs," I sniffled into the phone.

"Cass?" he asked worriedly. "What's wrong? Do I need to kick my brother's ass?"

"No," I whispered brokenly. "But can you please go and check on him? I'm worried about him."

"Cass...." He said the confusion clear in his deep voice.

"Please," I whispered. I could hear him standing up and then his truck keys jingle as a door shut.

"Yea," he said. "I'm on my way. Where is he?"

"He came by here on the way home from Nashville," I said biting my lip. "Things didn't go well. I'm sure he headed home."

"Ok Cassie," Kolby said with a sigh. "I'll check on him and let you know."

I'm Gone: Part I

B rantley's POV

I stared off into the darkness as I heard my front door slam. Fuck, I thought rubbing my face and taking another drag of my cigarette. I did not want any company right now. I sank further into the rocking chair on my back deck and wished whoever it was would just leave. Then I sat up a little holding out hope as I listened to the footsteps come through the house.

Maybe it was Cassie. Lord, please. Let it be Cassie. The footsteps reached the door for the deck and it swung open. I glanced over then my heart fell as I saw my brother making his way outside with a solemn look on his face. I tamped down the hurt, anger, and disappointment when he pulled up the chair beside me. We both sat there quietly for a few minutes listening to the sounds of the summer night.

"What are you doing here?" I murmured lightening up another cigarette. The nicotine was the only thing keeping the craving for a drink away right now. I wanted to get lost and forget the hurt. But I knew that if I started, I wouldn't stop this time. I had worked too hard to not be that guy.

"Cassie called me," Kolby said looking at me out of the corner of his eye as he lit his own cigarette. "Said things didn't go too well and she was worried about you. What's going on B?"

"We ended things tonight," I said not looking at him and sighing. "It just wasn't working Kolby. Neither of us were putting our relationship first. I really want to be pissed off at her, but man, I am just as guilty. I guess she called you because she was worried about what I would do."

"Yea man," my brother said quietly. "She did. She was right to, you know."

"I know," I said looking down at my hands and nodding. "I'm holding on by a thread man, but I'm not gonna do it. Because Kolby, I'm not giving up on her. I'm not giving up on us. And as much as I want to drown myself, I'd lose her for good for sure if I go down that road. I also do not want to be that guy again. I'll just find some other way to deal with it. Pills and booze are not gonna be the answer."

"Bro give her a little time," Kolby said looking over at me. "You both have been burning the candles at both ends. Hell, I saw her a few weeks ago when she wrapped this season and came by to see Mama. She looked so damn tired. Maybe....."

"Not right now man," I said holding up a hand to stop him. "I just can't talk about this right now. I don't see our lives changing any time soon. Maybe one day, but not right now."

May 2014

Brantley's POV

I shook the hand of the last reporter walking out of the Jefferson High gym and let out a deep breath as I walked to my truck. Rich walked by clapping me on the back giving me a wink. Coming home to do this album launch had been a great idea. I had never been more excited about an album than I was this one.

The new single with Justin and Thomas on it had hit radio today and I was excited to do the video next week. I pulled my phone out of my pocket along with my keys then unlocked my screen. I stopped in my tracks when I noticed the date.

Shit. I jerked my head up looking around the parking lot. Ben glanced over at me like he realized the same thing that I did. We had been so busy getting everything started and then with the tour kicking off. He pushed his shades up and made his way over to me as I leaned against the side of my truck.

"You heard from her?" I asked quietly. I knew he always did everything he could to make sure that Cassie wasn't alone on the anniversary of her parents death. Year before last I had flown to L.A. for her and last year Ben and I both had made sure she was on the road with us.

"No," Ben said with a sigh. "She got her early copy of the album a few weeks ago. Hasn't exactly spoken to me since then. I think she said something about getting Kelsey to go away with her. She's done filming for a few months and said she wanted to be nowhere near the state of Georgia this weekend."

"Why's she pissed off at you?" I asked giving him a funny look. He looked at me and rolled his eyes.

"Because apparently," he grumbled. "I should have warned her about "I'm Gone".

"So," I said shrugging my shoulders. "Not like it isn't true. She knows that I write what I know. Hell Ben, "17 Again" and "Let It Ride" are about her too."I had very vivid memories about the inspiration for those songs. I could still feel her soft skin under my fingertips.

"Yea B," Ben said shaking his head and smirking. "But that one is blatantly obvious. Not to mention the string of cuss words I heard when the video for "Bottoms Up" premiered. I think Shane even got a piece of her mind because he had originally asked her to be in it."

"I guess so," I said sighing in defeat. "Damn man. I miss her so fucking much. I tried to go by the set last time I was home. She wouldn't let me past the gate."

"Wellllll....." Ben drawled narrowing his eyes at me. "The date with Jana Kramer a few months back didn't help you any buddy. You know Cassie can't stand her ass."

"Man," I growled clenching my fists. "I told you a million times. That was a fucking set up. She cornered me. Like it was any better for me to get blasted with photos of her walking the red carpet to present at the Oscars on Scott Eastwood's arm."

"Well then get off your ass and do something about it," Ben growled back at me. "You still love her?"

"What kind of question is that?" I huffed yanking open my truck door climbing in. "I never stopped."

"Then you going to do anything?" Ben challenged as I shut the door and rolled the tinted window down to look at him shaking my head. "What the hell BG! Can't be chicken shit the rest of your life!"

"Not being chicken shit," I growled starting the truck. "It's called biding my time!"

I pulled out of the parking lot and turned to head out of town. I wasn't ready to go home to that empty house right now. I still even almost a year later, saw Cassie everywhere I looked in the damn thing. I snuck a glance over at my phone in the console and debating calling her to just see if she would answer.

I knew she didn't handle today well and I was worried about her. We hadn't talked since I left that night. I had caught a brief glimpse of her at the ACM's this year because she had been asked to present. But she had left as soon as she was done not sticking around. I'd had to answer to a seriously pissed off Caroline like it was my fault or something.

She still came to see Mama when she could but always made sure I was out of town. Which had been a lot.

I was so lost in my thoughts I didn't even realize it had grown dark. I sighed and turned around knowing I needed to head home. I jerked the wheel and almost ran off the road when my phone rang startling me. I picked it up and my eyes widened in surprise at the number. I quickly answered it and my heart stopped at the voice on the other end of the line.

"Hello," I said quietly gripping the steering wheel. I prayed I wasn't dreaming.

"B," I heard Cassie's quiet voice slur on the other end of the line. She quietly sniffled in my ear. I could tell she had been crying and possibly drinking a little. I need you."

"Cass, honey," I said softly pulling over to the side of the road my heart pounding in my chest. "Where are you?"

"I'm at the house," she mumbled. "I just....um.....maybe I shouldn't have called."

"I'm on my way," I said turning around and pointing my truck towards Athens. I gunned it. "I'll be there soon ok."

I'm Gone: Part II

<hr>

B rantley's POV

I pushed my truck to see just how fast I could get there. I drummed my fingers on the steering wheel at each red light that seemed to take forever. I almost called Ben to tell him what was going on, but stopped in the middle of dialing. No, she called me. She had said she needed me.

I pulled into Cassie's driveway and killed the engine climbing out. I ran to the front door and stopped when I realized it was locked. I tugged my keys out of my pocket and sure enough my key still worked. I unlocked the door stepping into the darkened house. I could hear the TV playing quietly and make out that the lamp by the couch was on. I kicked my boots off out of habit and sat my keys and hat down on the table by the door before quietly making my way into the living room. I stopped in my tracks at the sight before me.

Cassie had a couple of old photo albums scattered around on the coffee table along with tissues everywhere. One empty bottle of her favorite red wine was in the middle with what looked like another sitting by a glass half full. She was curled up in a ball, her knees pulled up to her chest sobbing.

I quietly walked forward and dropped down to my knees by the couch. I reached a big hand up and softly brushed the dark hair away from her face.

"Cass, " I whispered making her blink her eyes open to look up at me. She was startled at first when her bleary eyes focused on me then a fresh round of tears brimmed over. She lifted a hand to my cheek making me lean into it.

"Am I dreaming?" she murmured as I wiped a tear off her cheek. I could see the dark circles under her eyes and just how exhausted she must be. They did a great job at hiding them for her.

The boys and I never missed an episode. Thomas had been giving Lauren and I both hell last weekend because we went to go eat mad as hell over something that had happened on the show. I'd smacked him and said she may not be mine anymore, but I was proud as hell of her.

"No honey you're not," I whispered kissing the palm of her hand. "You called me."

"B, it hurts so bad," she slurred putting a hand right over her heart. "I miss them so much."

I leaned down scooping her up then settling back onto the couch with her in my arms. I stretched out with her buried into my side as she sobbed. I did my best to soothe her, but other than holding her I was at a loss at what to do. We'd kept her busy the last two years to keep her mind off it.

"I know you do baby," I murmured kissing the top of her head. "I know. There anything I can do?"

"Hold me," she whispered clinging to me trying to get closer. "I'm just so tired. I can't sleep."

"Just close your eyes Cass," I said playing with the ends of her hair. God, the feel of having her this close after so much time was killing me. I missed her more than I wanted to let anyone know at times. "I know today always gets to you."

"No Brantley," she slurred lifting her head to look down at me. She bit her full bottom lip as she toyed with the ends of my necklace. "It's more than just today. I can't sleep without you. Not unless I've worked until the point that I am exhausted or taken the sleeping pills the doctor suggested. I just can't. Breaks my heart all over again when I roll over to find you not there."

"Baby," I murmured with a sigh pushing a strand of hair behind her ear. "Come here."

"No," she whispered pushing off my chest and standing up. She reached for the glass and turned it up.

"Cassie," I growled standing up. I gently reached over to pull the now empty glass out of her hand. I wrapped an arm around her pulling her to me. "I'm speaking from experience honey, that's not gonna help."

"Why not?" she grumbled burying her face into my chest and fisting the back of my t-shirt in her hands. Cassie pressed as close to me as she could get making me moan low in my throat "This is all a dream anyhow. Please, please let me enjoy it."

"Baby," I growled fisting my hands in her dark hair pulling her head back to look at me. I lowered my head to brush my lips against hers. I bit her lip making her whimper and cling to me. "Does that feel like a dream?"

"Yes, no, hell, I don't know," she mumbled standing on her tip toes to claim my lips with hers. I picked her up wrapping her around me as she deepened the kiss almost making my knees buckle. Cassie had never completely understood just how quickly she could bring me to my knees.

I turned and walked towards her bedroom pushing her against the wall beside her door making her gasp. She yanked my shirt over my head latching her lips onto my throat as she slid her hand down my stomach to grasp my belt. I rocked against her letting her feel just how hard she made me then my eyes popped open as a moment of clarity hit. I wrapped a hand around her wrist stilling her movement.

"Cass," I said making her blink her eyes against the buzz and exhaustion I saw there. "Honey, stop."

"Why?" she snapped unlocking her legs from my waist and pushing me back. "I want you and you sure as hell want me! That hasn't changed. Why not just go with it? It's just sex B."

"It's never been just sex between us," I growled pointing a finger at her. She was blinking back tears and she tried to push past me stumbling but I grabbed her arm spinning her back around into my arms. "And you fucking know that Cassie. You may have tried to stop feeling something for me, but dammit I still love you."

"Really," she said balling her fist up to hit my chest as tears started to fall again. "You want to accuse me of not loving you anymore Brantley. I never fucking stopped! I don't think I ever will, which is why I am like I am right now. It hurts. So damn bad. But I can't find a way to make it work."

Her legs gave out on her as she sobbed. I picked her up and walked into her room laying her down on the bed before crawling in beside her.

"I can't either Cass," I murmured pulling her to me. I rolled to my side as she buried her face into my neck. I could feel the tears as she cried. "Lord knows, I've tried everything I can think of to find an answer."

I felt a shuddering sigh from her as I placed a soft kiss on her forehead. A second later I felt her breathing even out knowing she was asleep. I moved away slowly and stood up to kick my jeans off. Cass let out a quiet whimper and reached her hand out. I pulled the covers back and tugged her over to me as she buried her head into my neck and drifted back off. I settled the covers over us and felt my own eyes grow heavy.

I just wish I knew what to do to fix things. This is right where I wanted to be, but couldnt always be. Cassie shifted in her sleep and I felt something press into my shoulder. I moved back a little and rubbed the edge of her t-shirt sleeve feeling a lump under it. I gently slid a finger into the collar of her shirt and my eyes widened at what I found.

I slowly pulled the chain she had hidden under her shirt out and saw her ring still around her neck. I quickly replaced it as she whimpered in her sleep and felt my heart lighten just a little. She hasn't removed it from the last place I had put it. I held out a little hope that things maybe would be okay one day.

Cassie's POV

I jerked awake as my cellphone rang loudly from my nightstand. I sat up too quickly and felt the world start to spin. Dammit, why had I hit the bottle of wine so damn hard last night. I knew better. I should have kept my plans and went out of town with Kelsey like I had planned. I had just been so damn tired.

I couldn't even fathom getting on a plane or packing a suitcase. I almost called Ben to see what he was up to but remembered that they were on tour. Wasn't like I could call Brantley no matter how much I wanted to. I had given up the right the night I took my ring off my finger. I blinked my eyes against the bright sunlight and could tell they were puffy from crying.

How the hell had I gotten to bed last night? I glanced over at the clock groaning when I saw it was two in the afternoon. I never slept this late. My eyes widened a little at the bottle of water and Tylenol that was sitting beside my phone. Well, at least it looked like I had tried to prepare myself. I reached for them taking them quickly and then grabbed my phone.

I scrolled through the ton of text messages and emails. My eyes narrowed at the 911 from my agent. I clicked open the link she had sent me asking what the hell. According to TMZ, a local college kid had found my house here in Athens and noticed a familiar truck parked in the driveway.

I snorted and rolled my eyes as I climbed slowly out of bed because of my pounding head. I texted her back as I padded into the living room, to clean up the mess I had surely left, that it was a crock of shit. I hadn't talked to Brantley in almost a year. She knew that.

Oh, I had wanted to call. I had lost count of how many times my finger had hovered over his name but never pushed the button. I stopped when I noticed the absence of the wine bottles I know I emptied last night were replaced on the coffee table by a dozen of my favorite coral colored roses. My heart sped up as I looked around the house and stepped over to pick up the note attached to them. I let out a gasp as I started to read. My knees buckled, and I collapsed onto the couch.

Cassie,

I'm sorry that I wasn't there this morning. I had to be back to catch the bus heading to the next tour stop. As upset as you were, I hated the thought of you waking up alone, but I had no choice. Like always in our lives, duty called. Baby, please don't forget that no matter how much time has passed between us, I am here for you if you need me. Don't ever hesitate to call. I'll do everything in my power to help. I love you Cass. I told you I wasn't giving up and I meant it. Get some rest if you can.

Love Always,

Brantley

I wiped at the tears streaming down my face and reached up to touch my lips. It really wasn't a dream. He had been here. I really had called him. I wiped at my eyes as last night started to come back to me. I had called, and he was here. Dropped whatever it was he was doing and came because I needed him. I gritted my teeth against the tears not wanting to let myself read too much into it. He knew what yesterday was and how hard it was. But reading his words, I still held out a little hope.

Go Dawgs!

O ctober 2014

Cassie's POV

I looked in the mirror one last time checking my makeup and grinned. I had on my favorite Dawgs jersey with a pair of black skinny jeans and my red Converses. I'd left my long hair down and curled the ends. I had the weekend off from filming and tonight was the UGA homecoming game. Caroline and Luke were in town and had gotten a box to watch with a few friends.

Even though Brantley and I had been split up for over a year, I had still kept up my friendship with Caroline. She had begged me to fly out for some of Luke's stadium shows this summer, but I had refused because she had always planned for the ones Brantley was at. I had shaken my finger at her telling her I knew what she was doing.

I heard the honk of a horn in my driveway and grabbed my phone and wristlet before darting out the door. Caroline waved at me from the drivers seat of Luke's truck. I paused for half a second at the blonde in the passenger seat but smiled when recognition hit. I opened the back door climbing in and leaned over the console to give Caroline a big hug and smacking kiss on the cheek.

"Well damn Cass," Caroline said with a wink. "If being single this long is making you swing that way I just may have to divorce Luke. I bet you snore less."

"Please," I said with a laugh pushing her arm. "You love that man too much. I can't quite shake it for you like he can."

"Aghhh," Lauren groaned from beside me as I turned to wrap her in a hug. "Please do not get her started on the merit of Luke's assets. I may just puke."

"I agree," the woman in the front said with a laugh earning a smack from Caroline before she pulled out of my driveway. "We all see just how tight those jeans are. I'm Brittany."

"Cassie," I said giving her a grin then smirked. "I do believe that man of yours rocks some pretty tight jeans as well."

"Good God does he!" Caroline said fanning herself as she turned into the stadium parking lot. "I've been trying to bounce a quarter off Jason's ass for years."

"Woman!" Lauren said as we all cracked up. "For once in your life behave yourself."

"Not possible!" Brittany and I both said between laughs.

"What???" Caroline huffed as she parked the truck climbed out. She looped an arm around my shoulders as we headed into the stadium. "Ok Cass..... Spill."

"Spill what Caroline?" I asked pulling my ticket out of my pocket.

"Oh shit," I heard Brittany murmur. I gave her a funny look but got one in return telling me I was on my own with this one.

"Crap," Lauren said shaking her head and looking heavenward. "I knew this was coming. After that last concert, I knew this was coming. Half drunk and whipped the ruler out on the poor man."

"What?" I said narrowing my eyes as Caroline smirked and pointed towards the elevator we needed to take.

"Well, you've got to get back on the horse at some point so to speak honey," Caroline said giving me a wide smile. "I need to know what your measurement requirements are so I can help a sister out."

"Shiitttt...." Brittany squeaked.

"My what...."I asked whirling my head around with wide eyes. "Caroline? Are you asking me what dick size I prefer? First of all, I am not dating! Let alone sleeping with anyone. I don't have time."

"Pretty sure she's asking about just one in particular?" Lauren whistled out trying to not laugh.

"I just want to make sure you are getting what you are used to sweetie," Caroline drawled with a wide smile. I narrowed my eyes and raised an eyebrow at her.

"Caroline, are you trying to ask how big a certain person is?" I asked through gritted teeth shaking my head at her. Bless Luke, poor man had his hands full.

"That's exactly what she is asking," Brittany said with a snort. "She tried to get measurements with a damn ruler this summer. BG tried to climb PJ to get away from her."

My jaw dropped as Caroline whipped said ruler out of her bag with an evil grin.

"Now Cass," she said trying to keep a laugh in. "You don't have to say anything honey. You can just show us. Because sweetie, I know with that strut and that smirk, that man is packing."

"Caroline!" I yelped pushing her shoulders then cracked up laughing. We all piled out of the elevator headed to our box with a laugh. I didn't worry about drawing anyone's eye as we walked. I knew that the men these three were with would catch attention way before I would. I felt a little bit of envy towards them. They all had what I'd had but could actually make it work.

I shook off the melancholy feeling and followed Caroline over to the bar on the back wall to fix a drink. I had turned my head to listen as Lauren asked Brittany how the wedding planning was coming along, and I saw a familiar figure out of the corner of my eye. No, surely not. Caroline wouldn't do that to me.

"Caroline Boyer Bryan," I growled under my breath grabbing her arm pulling her over to a corner. I could see Brantley glaring at Luke who was raising his hands up in defense. "What the hell?"

"What Cass?" Caroline said batting her big blue eyes at me innocently. "I said it was friends hanging out. You knew the boys would spend time watching the game while we gossiped and yelled at the refs."

"But you didn't tell me he would be here," I grumbled cutting my eyes over to a glaring Brantley who was growling at Luke as Jason laughed. "You know we haven't seen each other."

Caroline leaned closer to me and grinned poking a finger into my shoulder. "That's bullshit sweetie. Everyone knows his truck was in your driveway a few months ago," she said giving me a look.

"And I just got the gossip columns to shut up about it," I snapped then sighed. "It was the anniversary of my parents death Caroline."

"I know honey," she said squeezing my arm." He told me. If it bothers you that bad I can take you back."

"No," I said sighing with a shrug. "I don't get to see y'all near about as much as I would like. I can handle it."

Brantley's POV

I was helping Thomas tweak a lyric for a song idea he had just before the game kicked off. We were sitting in the seats outside the box shooting the shit. It felt good to finally have a little down time. It had been a while since I'd slowed down long enough to go to a game so when Luke had called I had been all for it. I had asked where the girls were at when I arrived, but Luke had shrugged saying they had taken his truck to go pick something up.

I didn't think anything of it until we walked back in and I looked across the room to see Cassie standing there. I stopped so fast in the doorway Thomas, who was texting on his phone, ran into my back.

"What the hell BG?" he mumbled taking a sip of his beer then looked over my shoulder. "Oh shit."

"Luke," I growled under my breath and cracking my knuckles. "What the hell man? You said it was just a group of friends hanging out."

"What?" Luke said looking around then over at the girls. "Oh yea.....um mm...."

"Ahhh," Jason said with a wide smirk earning an elbow from me. "This ought to make the game even more interesting."

"BG, man," Luke said holding his hands up as I glared at him. "I didn't lie buddy. I can't help it that she and my wife are friends."

"A little warning would have been nice," I grumbled then looked over to meet Cassie's eyes. I nodded my head at her as she gave me a small smile before turning back to the conversation with Lauren. I stood still just watching her as she threw her head back laughing at something Caroline said. I turned on my heel and walked back outside to sit down. Luke followed me a moment later and leaned back in his chair propping his longs legs on the railing in front of us.

"You ok man," he asked looking over at me. I leaned forward bracing my elbows on my knees and nodded my head.

"Yea," I said quietly as we watched the teams warm up. "Just threw me for a second seeing her. But she's got as much of right to be here as I do."

"Man," Luke said taking a sip of his beer then looking at me. "If you miss her so damn much why don't you tell her?"

"Because nothing has changed," I said shaking my head. "We both are still just as busy, hell if not busier than we were. It wasn't that we didn't love each other man. We just couldn't make the time for each other."

"No, you just didn't want to," Luke said giving me a knowing look. "I know all about that. So, do Jason and Thomas. I know that with the two of you things are a little different because her career is just as demanding, but it's all about finding that balance. Just have to want it and then figure it out."

"We gonna sit around and talk about our feelings all night," Thomas said jumping over the back of the seat by me and settling in. "Or are we gonna watch the Dawgs kick some Tiger ass!"

Jason gave me a smirk and tossed me a bottle of water as he kicked back in the seat by Luke.

"Damn right," he muttered with a grin. "Let's watch some football."

Thomas leaned closer to me and turned the camera around on his phone with evil grin then flipped the camera off and I followed suit.

"What was that for?" I asked with a laugh as he furiously started typing.

"Sending that to Justin with the caption of Go Dawgs," he said cracking up.

"Oh lord," I heard behind us. I turned my head to see Lauren leaning over the railing with a grin. "Let the shit talking begin."

"Damn right," I said with a laugh.

Later on during the third quarter I had gotten a call from Mama letting me know that she had made it Indiana just fine. I was reading a text and looking at my phone as I walked back through the box and ran into someone. I heard a yelp and shoved my phone in my pocket then reached out to catch them from falling.

"Dammit B," I heard grumbled and looked down into a pair of glaring brown eyes. "Watch where your big ass is going. Run a woman over why don't ya."

"Well darlin," I said tightening my grip on Cassie's arms and smirked at her. "I can't help it if you have always falling at my feet."

"Pfttt...." She said rolling her eyes and then smiled patting my chest. "Keep telling yourself that hotshot."

Out of habit I reached over to tuck a strand of hair that had fallen across her face. Cassie sucked in a breath as my hand brushed her cheek. I kept it there as she looked up at me.

"You been doing ok?" I asked quietly. I hadn't seen or heard from her since that night in May.

"Yea," she said giving me a soft smile. "Thank you for that by the way."

"I meant what I said Cass," I said leaning closer. "Anytime you need me, call."

I leaned over and pressed a soft kiss to the corner of her mouth. Damn, the smell of her perfume was driving me crazy. Even if all I got was these couple of minutes alone with her I owed Caroline for her scheming. I heard a whimper low in her throat as I pulled back. She spun on her heel taking a couple of steps then stopped with her back to me. Cassie turned her head slightly looking at me over her shoulder.

"Brantley," she said quietly. I almost didnt hear her over the roar of the crowd outside. I walked forward and stood behind her as she leaned back into my chest. I lifted my hand to brush her curtain of dark hair away from her neck leaning over to nuzzle my chin against her neck.

"Yes," I rasped into her ear. I felt Cassie suck in a breath.

"I need you," she whispered as I wrapped an arm around her pulling her tighter to me.

"What do you want?" I asked biting down gently on the curve of her neck making her shiver.

"Take me home," Cassie said linking her fingers with mine. "I don't want to be alone tonight."

"That all you want?" I asked chuckling darkly in her ear earning me an elbow to the ribs as I spun her around draping my arm around her shoulders.

"If I have to spell it out to you hotshot," she grumbled pushing the button for the elevator. "Then you are getting rusty in your old age."

"I'll show you old woman," I growled as the doors opened and I shoved her in making her laugh as I backed her into the corner. "Just you wait."

Group POV

"Ha Thomas Luther!" Caroline said with a laugh smacking Luke in the chest after looking over her shoulder. "Pay up! I was right!"

"Dammit Caroline," he grumbled glaring at her as Jason laughed. "I hate it when you are right."

"That's just because you can't stand to lose," Lauren said lifting her head from Thomas's shoulder smirking at him. Luke flipped her off and sipped his beer. Jason laughed at Brittany fanning herself as they all watched the elevator doors slide shut.

"Damn," she said chugging her drink. "Y'all were not playing when you said all it would take is getting them in the same room and sparks would fly."

"Why they deny it I will never know," Jason said shaking his head and kissing her cheek.

"Because they are a pair of chicken shits," Caroline grumbled and crossed her arms. "One of these days."

"Caroline," Luke said covering his eyes and groaning. "You've had your fun meddling now leave them alone. Hell, I'm pretty sure they are off to a good start even before they reach the parking lot."

Pushing Buttons

C assie's POV

I bit my lip as I backed up to a corner of the elevator as far as I could go. My heart was pounding in my chest as I looked over at the man stalking towards me. He stilled when the doors opened again, and a group of older ladies piled in.

Brantley moved to the opposite corner and leaned against it tugging his hat down over his eyes. I snickered and lowered my head, so my hair would fall around it. They excitedly shifted around, and he stepped closer to me to make room for more people to get on when the elevator stopped again. I turned to the side and stood up on my tip toes to whisper in his ear.

"Where did you park?" I asked hearing him suck in a breath when my lips brushed his ear. He turned his head to look at me.

"By Jason," he said quietly. I nodded my head and leaned against his shoulder as the elevator reached the ground floor and everyone made their way out. Brantley laced his fingers through mine and tugged me behind him towards his truck. I climbed in after he opened the door and closed it behind me. I smirked and flipped the console up sliding over to the middle making him grin and shake his head when he climbed into the driver's seat.

He put the truck in drive and settled his hand on my knee as we headed towards my house neither of us saying a word. Leaning my head against his shoulder, I paused for a second unsure of what I was getting myself into. But then I took in the backwards hat out of the corner of my eye and thought about the smirk I had seen there earlier.

Most of all I thought about the desire I saw in those green eyes. Something I had seen the very first night I had met him. Knowing that it was still there for me was a very powerful thing. He pulled in my driveway cutting the lights and killing the engine sitting there quietly.

"Cassie," he murmured turning to face me.

"B," I said stopping him with a hand on his arm. "Can we just for one night not talk? I don't know how things will be when tomorrow comes, but I just want to feel. I'm tired of burying how much I miss you. The only thing I am sure of right now is that I want you."

"Cass honey," he sighed looking into my eyes. I shook my head moving over to climb in his lap. I wrapped my arms around his neck tugging him closer and placing a deep kiss on his lips making him groan.

"Before you even think of trying to tell me no," I whispered in his ear before nipping the curve of his neck as he pushed his hands into the back pockets of my jeans gripping tight. I chuckled quietly at his harsh breathing and tugged an ear ring between my teeth. "I know that this is more than just about sex Brantley. My feelings for you haven't changed. I just don't have any answers to the millions of questions we both have right now."

I rocked my hips against his erection earning me a moan and a sharp pop on the ass as I pulled my head back to smirk down at him in challenge. I was met with a blazing stare. "So, what you gonna do about it outlaw?"

"For starters," he growled pushing the door open and sliding out with me in his arms. I wrapped my legs around this waist and held on reaching back to shut the truck door for him. "There is a wall I plan on pinning you against in there."

"Mmmm," I said with a wide grin as he pushed me against the front door and unlocked it with his key. "I think I like the sound of that. What else you got up your sleeve?"

"Someone is kinda frisky tonight," Brantley said throwing his head back laughing as he opened the door walking inside and kicking it closed with his boot.

"Damn right I am," I whispered unhooking my legs and sliding down pushing his back against the door taking him by surprise. I stood on my tip toes nipping his bottom lip as I reached for his belt.

"Cass," he hissed when he heard me tug it loose and toss it behind me.

"Yes...." I murmured giving him a wink and tugged his jersey over his head. My eyes widened as I leaned forward to brush my lips over the newest ink on his chest making him dig his fingers in my shoulders. "I swear, it's like unwrapping a present. There's always new ink."

"Baby," I heard him gasp out as I kissed my way across his chest. "I've only got so much control honey and you are testing it."

"Hmmm," I purred slowly sliding my hand down his stomach flicking the button of his jeans open with my thumb and gently pulling the zipper down. If it had been any other time I may have been laughing because I could feel his knees trembling. I slipped my hand into the parted denim wrapping my hand around his hard as steel cock gliding it up and down gently.

"Fuck!" I heard growled and as soon as the smirk came across my lips I knew I had pushed the buttons too far. I barely registered being spun around and shoved against the door with a gasp. The coolness of the wood against my flushed cheeks. I moaned as a big hand slid under my own jersey and slipped under my bra to palm an aching breast.

"Wanna play sweetheart?" I heard growled in my ear as he pressed against me. "Two can play that game baby. "

He stepped back slightly tugging my shirt off then pushed me back into the door popping the hook on my bra and yanking it down my arms. I leaned my head back against his shoulders as he sank his teeth in my neck wrapping his arms around me and tracing his hands across my stomach to the top of my jeans.

He let out a dark chuckle making my knees wobble as he popped the button and eased the zipper down. I whimpered closing my eyes resting my forehead against the door he slid a long finger under the lace of my underwear and kissed his way down my neck sucking my sweet spot. "Oh baby. Mmm....so damn wet. Just for me."

"Stop teasing me," I murmured pushing my ass back to grind against him. I felt Brantley's chest rumble with a groan his hold on me slipped slightly. I ducked under his arm and darted towards my room with a laugh as I heard him growl and his footsteps as he stalked after me. I hopped on one foot yanking my shoes off as I shoved my jeans after them.

I could hear boots thud on the floor and grinned as I looked over my shoulder at him coming after me. He tossed his hat across the room with a grin and kicked his jeans aside. I let out a gasp when he picked me up tossing me on the bed then pounced on me. I stretched out looking up at him, his eyes gleaming with desire. He braced his hands on either side of me looking down.

"Cassie baby," he whispered leaning down to bite my lip." It's not gonna be slow. I want you too damn bad."

"Do your worst outlaw," I said with a grin wrapping my arms around his neck tugging his lips down to mine. He gripped the edge of my lace underwear with a smirk. I heard a loud rip as he kissed me deeply and I pulled my head back as he wrapped my leg around his waist. "Hey those....." I was cut off when he slammed into me making me scream. "Oh god, fuck!"

"I'll answer to god if you want me to," he whispered with a grin as he gripped my hips picking up the pace sliding me across the bed with each thrust. I dug my nails in his shoulders as he buried his face into my neck pounding into me. "Dammit Cass. You feel so damn good."

"Been too fucking long," I moaned out sinking my teeth in and tugging on the ear closest to me. I lifted my hips along with him making him push deeper. "Harder B. I'm so damn close."

I slid my hands down his back digging my nails into his ass pulling him closer. He pulled his hips back and slammed into me hard making me scream, my eyes rolling back in my head as I went over the edge. I felt him stiffen as he threw his head back with a groan following me as shot hot ropes of cum inside me. My whole body went lax as Brantley dropped his head down onto my chest breathing heavy. I moaned again and felt myself tighten around him making him shudder.

"Fucking hell," he mumbled lifting his head to blink up at me. He rolled to his side slipping out of me making me whimper and pulled me closer kissing the top of my head as I burrowed into his side. "Damn have I missed you."

"I bet," I snickered with a yawn. "Better rest up. I've got plans for you buddy."

He slipped a hand under my chin lifting my head to kiss me deeply making me arch closer with a moan.

"Oh baby girl," he said breaking the kiss and winking at me as he rolled over caging me in with that big body and rocking his hips against me. "You haven't seen anything yet. You will be lucky if you can walk."

Let's Give Them Something To Talk About

C assie's POV

I rolled over sighing and grinning slightly when I felt how deliciously sore I was. I slid my hand over to the other pillow beside me. My eyes popped open when I realized it was empty of the man that should have been sound asleep there. I know I wore his ass out last night. I lifted up on my elbow pulling the sheet up and looked around.

I bit my lip against the tears and flopped back on the pillow as my phone started going crazy on the nightstand. I reached over to pick it up and my eyes grew huge at the tons of messages and notifications. I clicked on the link from my agent and swallowed deeply as I sat up pushing my hair off my face.

It had hit Twitter that someone had snapped a photo of Brantley and I walking off the elevator at the game last night hand in hand. Then another of him helping me climb in his truck. Shit, why couldnt they just leave us alone. I debated texting my agent back and I paused when I heard a throat clear making me jump.

I glanced up and saw Brantley leaning against the doorway of my bedroom with his arms crossed over his leather covered chest. I drank in the sight of his backwards hat, white t-shirt covered chest, black leather jacket, jeans, chains, and boots. I had to suck in a gasp to keep from drooling. He gave me a smirk as he read the desire in my eyes. He pushed off the door and sauntered over to me leaning over the bed kissing my lips distracting me as he snatched my phone out of my hand.

"Nope," he murmured against my lips. "Not today Cass. We will deal with it later ok." He pulled back kissing my forehead. "Thought I had left before you woke up again huh baby? No sweetheart, just ran home to swap out the truck for the bike. Now, get your ass up and get dressed woman. You're the one who wanted to live for the moment."

"But B," I mumbled biting my lip and reaching for my phone making him glare at me. "You know we have to deal with this. It's gonna get out of hand. Just let me answer those messages please."

"No mam," he playfully growled at me holding my phone up higher out of my reach. "Nope....uh uh. Not happening today. I'm giving us another twenty-four hour reprieve from all this. Nobody else's fucking business what is going on with us right now. Yes, my phone has been blowing up too baby. Agents, friends, family, fans, they all can kiss my ass right now. The only thing I am worried about right now is taking a ride with you. Now, get your ass up. And take my advice, don't open a text from Caroline. I was soooooo not prepared for the one I got earlier."

"Oh shit," I muttered covering my face and keeping a laugh in thinking about the conversation I had with her yesterday. "With that woman I can only imagine. Can't be any worse than what she asked in the elevator yesterday. Luke, God bless him, he has his hands full with her.'

I pushed up on my knees letting the sheet fall and trailed a finger up his chest making him bite his lip. "Now, you said ride hotshot. Just what kind of ride are you talking about?"

"Baby girl," he said trapping my hand in his and lifting it up to press a soft kiss to my knuckles then rolled his eyes. "Yes, Luke does. Damn woman chased me around with a ruler this summer. I woke up to a text from her saying she was glad I got you back in the saddle."

He gave me a wink then tugged me out of the bed. Brantley placed a soft kiss to my shoulder then pushed me towards my closest. "Bike ride first baby, then..the other can be negotiated."

I turned and grabbed the edge of his beard tugging his head down kissing him deeply as I pressed against him. "Hmmm..... I'm afraid I just may have to insist on the other later." He popped my ass with a chuckle as I turned and headed to my closet. I paused at the door with a grin.

" I bet that was a sight. Her chasing you with a ruler. At least she didn't ask you what dick size you preferred like she did me in front of Lauren and Brittany."

He barked out a loud laugh as I turned to step into my closet grabbing a tight pair of jeans and slipping them on.

"Are you fucking kidding me?" he grumbled standing there watching me shaking his head. "You know what, never mind. I'm not surprised." He narrowed his eyes as he watched me zip up my jeans and slip a red lace bra on. I smirked at him as I pulled a gray long sleeve t-shirt on over it.

"Woman, you expect me to be able to enjoy a bike ride knowing you have nothing on under those tight ass jeans."

I blew a kiss at him and laughed as I leaned over to pull on a pair of socks and dig out my motorcycle boots he had bought me. I arched an eyebrow at him.

"Really outlaw," I sassed back. "I see there's no sweatpants under those holey ass jeans. Like you are any more innocent."

"Baby," Brantley said smirking at me. "You got me there. But you and I both need this ride as much as we needed last night." He stepped over helping me shrug into my jacket wrapping his arms around me. "That was never our problem." He pulled my phone out of his pocket shaking it at me. "This was. We didn't turn these off enough and just be us. Now, enough of this shit. You ready sweetheart?"

He slipped my phone into his jacket pocket as his started to ring. He stilled then paled as he pulled it out of his pocket and I crossed my arms glaring at him.

"Shit," he mumbled rubbing his chin and staring at the screen. "That's Mama. I've got to answer it."

"Brantley Keith," I growled glaring at him then gasped as he switched it off mid ring. A second later mine started to ring. I tried to grab it but he pushed me back and cutting mine off too tucking it in his jacket. "B! you should have let me answer it. Now she's gonna kick my ass."

"Yea well," he grumbled pulling me to the door. "We are both gonna both be in dip shit for that. She must have seen the news."

Brantley opened the door then locked it behind us as we stepped out.

" Kolby set up Google alerts on her phone. Now any time either of our names pop up. Bam."

"Remind me to kick Kolby's ass," I muttered walking over his bike. "All we need now is Mama breathing down our necks. It's gonna be bad enough with the press and tabloids. She's still unhappy with me for ending our engagement. She hates seeing us apart. I know she means well, but I still feel guilty about hurting her along with you."

He grinned at me and held a big hand out to help me climb on the bike. He leaned over to kiss my lips gently and handed me my helmet.

"She's in Indiana baby," he muttered. "We have a little reprieve before she's back to raise hell. Guilt huh? That why you over there when I am out of town?"

"Not all of it," I said glaring at him. "You know I love that damn woman. Even though I get asked if I have come to my senses yet as soon as I walk in the door. Kolby is a dead man walking you hear me!"

He let out a loud laugh settling on in front of me slipping his helmet and shades on.

I hear you honey, he said as I wrapped my arms around him settling my head on his shoulder. "When he finds out you know about that he will be heading for the hills. And I know you love Mama, Cass. She knows it too?"

"What are we gonna tell her B?" I said sliding my hands under his jacket to grip his t-shirt. "You know she's gonna have questions."

"Baby," he said squeezing my hands then turning the key. I shivered and grinned as he started the bike. "Remember, our phones are off, and we are not talking about this for another twenty-four hours. You don't have to be back on set until Monday night, right?" I nodded my head. "Well then, let's go for a ride baby girl. Spend some time just the two of us ok?"

"Sounds like a plan outlaw," I said kissing his cheek making him grin as he took off out of my driveway. I laid my head on his shoulder just enjoying the feeling of being with him. Whatever else that was to come, we could figure it out later.

Yea... F That!

B rantley's POV

Early December 2014

I had my phone held in the crook of my neck as I tried to get all my gear stuffed in my backpack before we left to go for the evening hunt. I had been up in Illinois for almost a week with Michael Lee. This was one time I had been thankful to be able to be lost in the woods. Damn phone, email, social media, everything had been a shit storm for over the last month.

If I had to mutter no comment one more time, I just may hit someone. Even more fuel was added to the fire when I had shown up to the CMA's dateless last month. Didn't help that I stumbled over the question of whether Cassie and I were an item again a few times on the red carpet because Caroline and Luke were behind me and she kept mouthing "bullshit" at me.

Cassie and I both had agreed for now that it was our business and ours alone. We kept to ourselves as best we could. She came out to the house a good bit since everyone left me alone there. Mama had read us both the riot act when she had gotten home from Indiana and was still glaring over the fact we really didn't have an answer for her on what was going on.

"Brantley?" I heard Cassie snap in my ear. "Did you hear what I just said?"

"Sorry sweetheart," I answered looking around for my gloves. I had the damn things earlier. I felt something hit the back of my head and turned to glare at Michael laughing then picked my gloves up off the floor.

"Trying to get all my stuff together. Hang on one sec." I turned and walked out to sit on the porch taking a deep breath of the cold air and settling down in a chair kicking my booted feet up. "Ok, you have my undivided attention Cass."

"Must be nice to get away to the middle of nowhere," Cassie grumbled. I could hear her shuffling around in her dressing room.

"Baby," I said trying to cheer her up. "If you want I'll take you to the farm in Bama when I get back and you wrap things up until after the first of the year. Or anywhere you wanna go. As long as it involves you, a soft bed, and no people."

"Maybe," she says quietly.

"Cassie," I said leaning forward in my chair clueing in that something was up. "What's wrong?"

"Look B," Cassie says, and I can hear her tapping her nails on something near her. A nervous habit of hers. "Marsha and the producer for the show have come up with an idea."

"And what is that honey?" I asked through clenched teeth. I could tell right now that I wasn't going to like this at all.

"Umm well," she stuttered. "To quiet all the suspicion about us theyve set up a date between me and Josh tonight. Here in Atlanta."

"Do fucking what?" I snarled. "Let me repeat this to make sure I have it correct. They want you, to go out on a date with your co-star, so everyone will stop talking about us? I don't fucking think so! I'll get Rich on the phone right now to issue a damn statement!"

"Brantley Keith!" Cassie snapped back. "Don't you take that tone with me."

"Why in the hell would you think this is a good idea Cass?" I yelled. "Last time I checked it was my bed that you have been in!"

"I know," she grounded out. "But this is what fucked us up so bad last time. Putting a damn label on it. I thought we agreed not to for right now. Look it's just a date ok."

"Yes, I agreed to no labels because everyone was so concerned with what we were up to," I snapped. "I agreed because after a year without you, baby I am willing to take you any way I can. But now, you want my jealous, territorial, caveman tendency having ass to be ok with you going out without another man! One that I might add, everyone has already been speculating you were secretly dating since the show started. Even when you were engaged to me! FUCK THAT!"

"B!" she yelled. "Just calm down. It doesn't mean anything ok. Its just for show. You think I like having my movements tracked to see if I am headed to see you. No! I fucking hate it. I hate looking over my shoulder when I head out to Maysville to see if I am being followed. And heaven forbid if you even step foot in Atlanta. At this point I am willing to try anything to get both of us a little peace! We both live here! We aren't like everyone else and live in Nashville and L.A.! I stayed here in Athens, so I could still have a normal life, same as you!"

"Here's a bright idea sweetheart," I growled feeling my blood pressure rise. "How about you quit hiding that ring around your neck and let me put it back on your finger! That should make a big enough statement!"

"Brantley," Cassie growled. "We've talked about this."

"Yes," I grumbled. "We have. Or more so you've talked, and I listened. Mother fucker should have never come off your finger to begin with!"

"You know why it did!" she yelled back. I could hear the tears in her voice and I reached a hand up to rub my face in frustration.

"And near about killed me when you did it!" I seethed. "You know what Cass. Do what you want. Go out with him! If that's what you think is the best move for you, to hell with what I want! I'm just the man that loves you. But no, no, we can't talk about that! You know what I think, fuck what they all think. Let them guess! Better yet honey, if that's the way that things needed to be handled, if you need to go out with another man, then lose my fucking number!"

"Brant.." she got out before I cut the call and powered down my phone. Together officially or not, if she thought I would be ok with her going out with someone else, when she's in my bed and my ring still on a chain around her neck, she had another thing coming.

I stomped inside grabbing my stuff and my rifle and stalked out to the side by side to wait on Michael to come on and load up. He came out a few minutes later giving me a wary look. I was pretty sure he could see the steam coming out of my ears as I puffed on my cigarette.

"Everything ok?" he asked looking at me intently. "Think half the state heard that argument with Cassie."

"Nope, it's not. Far from it," I growled out then sighed. "But I don't want to talk about it. Let's go kill something. Maybe Maverick will walk out."

A few nights later I was sprawled out in my bed staring at the ceiling with my arms folded behind my head. I hadn't talked to Cassie since I had hung up on her the other day. I knew she was supposed to have finished filming until after the first of the year yesterday. I had gotten home from my hunting trip this evening. I had almost kept going on to Athens to confront her but thought better of it.

I thought about the year I had ahead and frowned. Maybe this blow up was for the better. I was going to be on the road a lot being on tour with Kenny. Not to mention being overseas right after the beginning of the year. I knew Cassie had a movie lined up to start filming in early January that would be done here other than a few days on location in Ireland. We both had been excited that it was around the same time I would be over there so she had planned to make that show.

It seemed despite our best intentions of giving this some time, it had blown up in our faces yet again. Loving each other wasn't the problem. It was finding the time for each other. I was turning thirty in about a month and I was getting to the point I was ready to slow down some. I shifted my leg under the covers trying to get comfortable.

The only thing I was sure of at this point as far as the future was that I wanted Cassie by my side. Her agreeing to this date made me wonder now, maybe she didn't want the same thing. I heard a noise downstairs and I glanced over at the clock seeing it was one in the morning.

I dropped my head back down on the pillow shaking my head. Probably just Kolby deciding to crash her for the night. My eyes blinked open as I heard footsteps hit the stairs and I remembered that Kolby was in Alabama hunting. I sat up putting my back against the headboard and reached for the pistol in my nightstand. My hand stilled on the butt of the gun when the footsteps stopped right outside my door. I heard the door crack open and I flicked the lamp on.

Cassie let out a squeak in surprise when she looked over to see me propped up in bed glaring with my pistol in my hand. She jumped back bumping into the door almost falling down.

"What the hell Cassie!" I snapped. "You could have been shot! Give a man some warning next time."

She closed the door and leaned against it biting her lip and blinking back tears at my harsh tone. Her long hair was tousled around her shoulders and she was wearing one of my long sleeve WWP t-shirts and pajama pants with a pair of slip on boots.

I could see the circles under her eyes and I knew she hadnt slept any better than I had the last few days. She gulped and lowered her eyes as she took in my glare. I was still so damn aggravated with her right now. She pushed off the door and turned to open it then looked back over her shoulder at me.

"I'm sorry Brantley," she said quietly. "I shouldn't have come out here." She bit her lip before continuing. "For what's it's worth B, I didn't go. I told Marsha I couldn't do that to you and to find another way. I'm gonna go. Let you get some sleep."

"Cassie," I called out with a sigh feeling my heart lighten a little at her words. "Come here."

She turned around to look at me as a tired smile spread across her face. Cassie kicked off her boots and walked to the side of the bed putting her phone and keys on the nightstand before crawling in beside me. I lifted the covers as she moved over burrowing into my side with a sigh. I wrapped an arm around her stroking the hair away from her face.

"B, I'm...." she said softly. I stopped her with a finger on her soft lips and a shake of my head as I reached back to cut the lamp off.

"Not tonight sweetheart," I murmured kissing her forehead. "Sleep. Let's just sleep." I looked down at her with a smirk. "Which is half the reason why you come strolling in here after midnight isn't it baby? You couldn't sleep. How did you know I was home?"

"Mama," she mumbled tangling her legs with mine and tucking her head into my shoulder tracing a finger on the tattoo on my chest. "She told me earlier when she called to ask me about going Christmas shopping. Said you were headed in and surprised that I didn't know. Then hounded me about what we were fighting about now. Said we both sounded like a pair of wounded, grouchy, grizzlies."

I let out a quiet chuckle as her eyes closed. "Yea, that sounds about like Mama,"I said with a sleepy smile.

"And no, I couldn't sleep," she whispered drowsily. "I need you to sleep. I just need you. Plain and simple."

"I know baby," I said heaving out a deep sigh. "I know."

Not even a minute later I felt her breathing even out as she fell asleep. I lay there watching her. I was exhausted myself but couldn't shut my mind off. Slightly afraid it wasn't there, I pushed Cassie's hair away from her neck making her whimper in her sleep and slipped a finger under the collar of my shirt.

I let out a quiet sigh of relief when I felt the thin chain. I gently tugged it out holding the ring in the palm of my hand. At least it was still there. From what she had told me, it hasn't left her neck since I put it there for her. I stared at it for a moment longer stroking my thumb over the cool metal and stone.

"Really wish you would let me put that back on your finger," I whispered more to myself than to the sleeping woman in my arms. "Where it belongs."

Five More Minutes.....Please

Cassie's POV

I let out a sigh snuggling back further into Brantley's chest. I could tell from behind my closed eye lids that it was daylight. Just wasn't sure what time. Not like I cared anyhow. I had no immediate plans other than to be right where I was at. I had sent Marsha an email last night before I headed over here that I was worn out and told her to cancel anything else I had until the first of the year.

I knew it was just a couple small interviews and an appointment to look at a couple of scripts. I hadn't known how things were going to go so I wanted to give myself some time if they had ended up in flames. Which, they still might. I smiled as I felt a big hand slide under the t-shirt I was wearing and a soft kiss pressed to the back of my neck causing me to shiver.

"Shut it down Cassie," Brantley mumbled sleepily burying his face in my hair shifting closer to me. "I can hear you thinking."

"B," I tried to argue then hissed out a gasp when he slid his hand further up pinching a nipple. "Ow."

"Then shut it down woman," he growled tightening his arms around me. "Before I spank your ass."

"Well now," we heard a voice say from the foot of the bed. "That's the best idea I have heard out of your mouth in a while son. Both of you need one at this point."

We both stilled and I slowly reached up to pull the gray comforter down and peered over it. Mama Becky was standing in the middle of the room with her arms crossed over her chest glaring at both of us. She had on the bright red oversize sweater I had bought her last time we went shopping with a pair of jeans. A pair of big sunglasses were perched on the top of her head.

Sylo was sitting at her feet watching both of us wagging his tail. I knew he wanted to jump up here in the middle of us but was waiting on a signal from either me or B. He must have stayed with her while Brantley was gone. I sat up quickly as Brantley stretched rolling his eyes. He sat up slowly and propped his chin on my shoulder raising his eyebrow at his mama. She pointed a finger back and forth between us.

"You two shit birds need to get your crap together," she grumbled as I gasped. "Even I am tired of the are they or aren't they."

"Mama," Brantley said with fake shock and an evil grin. Oh shit, don't get us in more trouble B, I thought closing my eyes. "You cussed! Better go pray!"

"Son," she growled. And here it was I thought he got that trait from Keith. "You may be almost thirty, but I can still tan your hide. I'm not the one in bed together and no ring on either of your fingers! Now get your butts up. I need help getting my tree and decorations down. I swear, y'all need to get it together. I want grand children before I am too old to enjoy them!"

"Mama," he said rolling his eyes then snapped his fingers for Sylo, who dove on the bed tackling me. He rolled over on his back for me to scratch his belly as I watched the two of them face off out of the corner of my eye. "We were just sleeping. You know that's the main thing you do in a bed."

"Brantley Keith," Mama Becky said rolling her eyes and shaking her head. "Son, I was born at night, but it wasn't last night. I know good and well if I had been about ten minutes later I wouldn't have walked in on innocent sleeping. I risked it anyways when I saw Cassie's car parked by your truck because I knew how tired both of you have been. Now, get your tails up!"

"Mama," we both whined. Sylo looked at her begging as well.

"But we are sooooo tired," Brantley said stretching with a wide fake yawn.

"Yea," I said batting my eyes leaning against his shoulder pouting. "And Sylo needs snuggles."

"You two have exactly one hour to be standing in my kitchen," she grumbled turning to walk out. She paused at the doorway and give us a smirk that could rival Brantley's on any day. "There's homemade soup and cornbread in it for both of you. But may want to get a move on. Kolby called that he's on his way back from Bama. Don't want to let him get to it first."

With that she walked out the door and down the stairs. We both looked at each other then kicked the covers back both of us pushing and shoving the other out of the way to get to the shower first. One did not play when it came to Mama's homemade soup and corn bread.

A couple hours later I walked into the kitchen shaking my head at the boys arguing over which way the tree needed to go in the living room. I paused as Mama Becky turned from the stove where she was fixing hot chocolate. She pointed a finger at the stool at the island and gave me a look.

Shit, I just got the mom look. I almost backed out to go hide behind Brantley. I pushed the sleeves of his sweatshirt up and shuffled over to sit down. She gave me a smile as she slid a mug over to me then braced her hands on the counter looking at me.

"Cassie honey," she said. "What are you doing?"

"Ummm...." I said looking around. "I'm sitting here Mama."

"Good lord," Mama Becky said rolling her eyes. "I don't know who tries to deflect the situation more. You or B." She walked picked up her own mug and walked around to sit beside me placing a hand on mine. "Y'all can't keep this back and forth up forever honey."

"I know Mama," I whispered looking down biting my lip. "We both stay so busy with work, it's hard."

"Baby," she said reaching up to push strand of hair that had fallen out of my messy bun out of the way. "And marriage is ten times harder than both of your careers put together. But you both have reached a point that y'all need to remind a couple of them they work for you, not the other way around. I know that things are kind of set in stone in some aspects for this next year. But keep it in mind for the future. You both love each other so much honey."

"More than I ever thought possible," I said looking over at her blinking back tears. "I'm terrified of losing him too."

"Sweetie," she said cupping my cheek with a wink. "That boy has had his heels dug in on you since the first moment he laid eyes on you. He's not going anywhere. Even if he's mad. I hadn't seen him smile that much over a girl in years. Did my heart good. And I love you like you are my own daughter. Y'all will figure it out. Just focus on each other."

"That's what I keep telling her," I heard Brantley say from the door way. He walked over leaning down wrapping his arms around me. I leaned into him with a sigh as he lowered his head kissing my cheek.

"Love you baby," he whispered. I could see Mama grinning out of the corner of my eye.

"Love you too B," I answered back lacing my fingers with his.

"Alright," Kolby called out walking in and grabbing a couple cookies off the plate in front of us. "We gonna keep the lovey dovey crap up all night you two or we going to decorate this tree."

I narrowed my eyes at Kolby remembering I owed him for teaching Mama Becky how to set up Google alerts. He paused mid chew as I let a low growl out making Brantley bark out a laugh. He creeped back around the island keeping a wary eye on me.

"Why does she sound like you right now BG?" Kolby asked growing pale. "What did I do?"

"Google alerts on Mama's phone," he answered with a laugh as I stood up pushing the stool back and reached for the wooden rolling pin Mama had left out earlier. "You made sure she'd be able to keep up with alllllllll the gossip about us now."

"Shit," he gulped. "Now Cassie honey......sweetheart."

"Run Kolby," I growled stomping towards him. "You better run."

He took off running with a yelp with me right behind him.

"Just don't dent my rolling pin on his hard head," Mama yelled after me as she started laughing.

"But Mama," Kolby yelled darting around the couch. "I'm your baby boy!"

"Tough!" she yelled back making me grin at him as I got closer shaking it at him. "She's my baby girl! That trumps you right now!"

Going Through The Big D....Maybe It Means Dallas

April 2015: 50th ACM Awards

Caroline's POV

I pasted one more bright smile on my face as the reporters snapped a couple more pictures of me and Luke. Finally, the end of the red carpet was in sight. I slid my hand under his suit jacket and calmly pinched him on the ass. He jerked but never broke his smile as he cut his eyes down at me. I grinned back up at him as he bit the inside of his cheek to keep from laughing.

"Baby," he mumbled tightening an arm around me. "You better quit."

"What?" I asked innocently as Luke looped my arm through his to help me towards the doors. We made our way over to Kerri who was talking to Cole. I paused to give BG a kiss on the cheek and a hug before following Luke. He went over a few things with Kerri before giving me a quick kiss and jogging off to get ready to kick the show off. Cole held his arm out to help escort me to my seat for the start of the show. I could hear a name being called at the end of the carpet making me stop. I tugged on Cole's arm and spun him around.

"What the hell Caroline?" he asked stumbling.

"Just a sec," I muttered seeing a long tan leg step out of the limo. I cut my eyes over to a familiar pair of leather jacket covered shoulders and smirked. I turned my head and batted my eyelashes at Cole. "Cole, sweetie I need you to do me a big favor tonight."

"What's that Caroline?" he said leaning his head a little closer, so he could hear me.

"Aww shit," I heard muttered by my left shoulder. "She's up to no good already."

I turned my head to give Brittany a wide grin. "Now what would give you that assumption?" I asked with fake innocence.

"Because you are always up to no good," she muttered, and I elbowed her in the side making her laugh as I watched Brantley track Cassie's every movement. Oh sure, he was hiding it, but to someone who knew the pair, it was very obvious.

"Oh, go back into your newlywed bubble," I snickered and rubbed my hands together before addressing Cole." Now, as you see Cole honey, Cassie is presenting an award tonight. Damn, he hasn't taken his eyes off her. Good thing he's wearing those dark sunglasses. Be giving them all more to gossip about with those fuck me eyes I know he's giving her."

"Good lord Caroline," Cole said with a booming laugh then crossing his arms looking at me. "Now what do you need me to do?"

"I need you to flirt with her handsome," I said giving him a big grin and kept my laugh in as he paled.

"Fuck no!" he hissed shaking his head as Brittany started laughing. "I don't have a death wish honey."

"Chicken," Brittany said covering it with a cough making me giggle.

"I'll kick your ass if you don't," I grumbled poking his shoulder. "Or a certain video from college may find its way onto Instagram."

"Dammit Caroline," he grumbled. "BG will kill me. Aren't they back together or something?"

"Or something," I said rolling my eyes. "While the official word is no comment."

"He's been too busy with touring," Brittany chimed in. "And she's been filming the show and a movie. That's if you ask either of them swear it's like listening to a broken record. But according to Twitter they've been seen together a few times since last fall."

"They are keeping it low key," I growled glaring at the back of Brantley's head then down the line at Cassie. Even from us. "If I hear I don't know what you are talking about Caroline one more time. Look Cole, she's going to be with me tonight, so I can keep him from killing you. I'm just talking a little innocent flirting. Knowing BG, it won't take too much more than smiling at her."

"Fine," he huffed as Jason walked up. "But you better keep him from killing me."

"What are you up to now Caroline?" I heard asked from behind me as we all turned to head inside. I leaned my head back and gave Cassie a dazzling smile. The dark green dress with the plunging neck line and thigh high slit looked amazing on her. The color set off her tan and dark hair.

"When am I ever up to something girlie?" I said sweetly making the guys crack up. She gave Brittany a hug and big kiss on the cheek before walking over to me.

"Because you always are," Jason said pulling Brittany into his side.

"Always thinking the worst of me," I said rolling my eyes and linking my arm with Cassies. "I am an angel."

"Oh Lord," Cole said looking up at the sky. "Better watch out for lightning. Good to see you again Cassie."

"You too," she said giving Cole a wide smile as we made our way inside to our seats.

We had gotten settled in when Cassie pulled her phone out of her purse, gasped, then turned bright red before she furiously sent back a reply. I couldn't keep the laugh in. Something told me I knew exactly what she had read. I leaned over trying to read but she covered it up turning redder.

"Asked you if you were wearing underwear under that dress, didn't he?" I whispered with a laugh.

"How the hell did you know that?" she hissed looking back over her shoulder shooting BG a look.

"Because I know you two," I said with a wink then kept in a laugh when Cole came by to see if we needed anything and leaned close to Cassie putting a hand on her shoulder giving her a smile. I covered a laugh with a cough because I am fairly sure I could hear a growl from two rows up even over all the noise.

Cassie's POV

I wound my way through the hallway in the stadium after I had finished my part on giving out the award for New Artist of the Year. I am sure Brantley had a lovely look on his face when Cole gave me a huge hug when he got on stage. I had been around him at a couple of Luke's shows and he was a sweet guy. I looked left and right dodging around people as I walked looking for Luke's dressing room because she was back here getting Carter to fix both of us a drink.

I turned a corner never seeing a door open and a long, leather covered arm snake out grabbing my wrist. I was yanked into the dark room the door slammed shut behind me. I blinked against the darkness but gasped when I felt a familiar pair of arms band around me pulling into his hard chest.

"Woman," Brantley growled into my ear ghosting a big hand across my stomach teasing the skin where my dress dipped in the front. He nipped my ear making me gasp. I noticed we were in one of the trainers rooms. "Give me one damn good reason I shouldn't bend your ass over this table and show you just why you are mine not anyone else's. If Cole so much as puts......"

I leaned further into his chest rubbing my ass against the hard tent in his jeans with a quiet laugh.

"B, I can't think of one damn good reason not to," I whispered huskily. "But I can think of several why you should."

I reached a hand back to rub his hard dick making his hiss. "And far as Cole, baby come on, you haven't figured out by now that is Caroline being up to no good. All she wants is a reaction out of you."

"I swear," he grumbled wrapping one arm tighter pulling me closer and pushing the hair off my neck with the other. I whimpered as he slowly placed wet, hot kisses from my shoulder up my neck swirling his tongue in the curve making me close my eyes and moan. "Luke needs to spank her ass one good time."

"Brantley, " I said with a quiet laugh. "Why do you think she does it?" I felt his chest rumble with a laugh as he bent his knees slightly and slide his hand down further finding the slit in my dress. I whimpered deep in my throat. "I'm gonna have to thank her for pushing your buttons this time though. It's been a long couple of months."

Chuckling deep in his chest he eased a hand inside my dress across my hot, bare, pussy. "Hmmm......" he hummed in appreciation sliding a calloused finger up and down my slit as I almost forgot how to breath as I arched my back giving him better access. Damn man knew how to play my body as well as he did a guitar. "Already wet for me baby. God knows, I have been hard enough to drive nails ever since I saw you in this dress. I swear you pick the ones designed to try and bring me to my knees."

"I.I.I...." I stuttered leaning my head back against his shoulder losing my breath as he pushed one finger in my wet slit sliding in and out before he added another. "Neeeeeedddddddd."

"Need what baby?" he murmured nuzzling my neck with his beard then biting softly under my chin never breaking his slow pace with his fingers. "Need me or need to cum?"

"Can't I have both?" I moaned out starting to tremble. I let out a gasp when he pulled his finger out then spun me around backing me into the wall. In the dim light from the hall I could see that dark smirk spread across his full lips. Before I could even register what was going on he had dropped to his knees in front of me pushing my dress up and exposing me to the cool air.

"Fuck yes," he chuckled leaning forward to flick his tongue against my clit. "I was right. No panties in sight. And oh baby, don't you taste so fucking sweet."

"B," I whimpered loudly as he brushed a knuckle against me making me arch my back more. I glanced down propping a hand on his jacket covered shoulder and almost came just from the look of desire on his face. We both had been too damn busy to see each other much lately.

"Baby, better be quiet unless you want to give all of country music a show," he whispered with a wink.

Then the damn man reached up turning that godforsaken hat backwards before sitting my right leg up on his shoulder opening me up further. He leaned forward diving face first nipping my clit then sucking it between his teeth as he eased a long finger in and out of my dripping pussy. "Oh god....." I moaned throwing my head back against the wall tightening my grip on his shoulder to keep my legs from buckling from the sensations.

Brantley paused and looked up at me with hooded eyes. He curled his finger inside me with a smirk then added a second one.

"Baby girl," he whispered looking up at me. "I have told you time and again hes not going to answer. But if you want to call me that I will gladly answer anything you need. Starting with this."

He buried his face back between my thighs swirling that long tongue around my engorged nub then curling his fingers in me and nipping my clit. I swear I saw stars.

"Bbbbbbbbbb..." I stuttered gasping as I started to tightening around his fingers going over the edge. "Brantley!" He eased fingers out of me as I whimpered from the loss of contact.

He trailed his tongue over my slit one more time making my legs buckle as he chuckled against me. He stood up quickly catching me. Brantley leaned down kissing me deeply and pressed me further into the wall as I sucked his tongue hard getting a taste of myself on him.

"Who said I was done with you darlin?" he mumbled against my lips as I pulled my head back to look at him in surprise.

"Well there is a show going on and someone is bond to come looking for one of us," I whispered leaning over to tug an ear ring between my teeth making him hiss.

"Yea..... we will get back to that," he said with a quiet laugh tugging me off the wall and spinning me around. "Eventually."

He shuffled me forward pushing me against the massage table there. Oh, fucking hell, was all I could think as he placed a soft kiss in the middle of my exposed back as he leaned over me. I heard the hiss of his zipper as I reached down to help him tug my dress up out of the way. He rubbed the head of his hard cock against my dripping folds before whispering in my ear. "Now, got to try and be quiet baby girl. "

I felt my eyes roll back into my head as he thrust forward hard making me lean further over the table and I couldnt help the loud moan that escaped my lips. I bit my lip as he picked up the pace to keep them in.

"Dammit to hell baby," he murmured leaning into me and muffling the words against my shoulder. "Fuck. You feel so damn good."

He squeezed my hips as he pounded into me. If I hadn't been in such a state of ecstasy at the moment the voices in the hallway may have given me pause.

"Britt? Have you see Cassie? I've got her drink right here" Caroline called out.

I looked back over my shoulder at the man behind me and whimpered at the sight of him gritting his teeth to keep his own moans quiet as I tightened him on purpose making him gasp. He reached forward wrapping an arm around my neck then slid his hand over my mouth to muffle a moan as he thrusted harder making the table move slightly. Brantley pulled me up flush against him and drove up hard in me.

"Cum now, "he growled in my ear as I tightened around him and he sank his teeth into my shoulder as I felt him shoot hot ropes of cum inside my whimpers muffled against his hand.

"PJ!" Caroline and Britt called from outside. Oh fuck, I thought as I came down from my euphoria. They were still out there. "Have you seen Cassie? We can't find her."

"Oh god," I grumbled out quietly as he lowered his hand. I whimpered as he slipped out of me and I felt him chuckle against my neck.

"Baby," he said brushing his lips along mine softly. "I already told you to call out my name." He zipped his jeans back up and fixed his belt then turned my around pulling me up in his arms kissing me deeply. He sat me back down onto wobbly legs then winked at me." May want to fix that lipstick honey, it's all gone."

I pushed up onto my tip toes because even my heels weren't tall enough tonight to help wrapping a hand into his t-shirt and yanked him closer kissing him then pulling back to nip his bottom lip.

"Mmmm...." I said reaching up to wipe the pink lipstick that was smeared around his lips away. "Thank you. I needed that baby and apparently so did you."

"Well," he murmured in my ear as he wrapped his arms around me as I looked in my hand mirror fixing my lipstick and smoothing my hair back into place. "If we weren't heading opposite directions as soon as this is over, I would find a soft bed somewhere so I could make love to you properly. I've missed you Cassie."

"I miss you too," I said turning around to bury my face in his chest hugging him tightly. "Now, the question is how are we going to get out of here hotshot."

"Umm well baby," he murmured looking bashful. Yea, he hasnt thought about that. "Ughhhh..."

We both jumped at the knock at the door.

"Shit," I said looking up at Brantley with wide eyes.

"Oh fuck," he mumbled turning a little pale. I tried to calm myself. So, what if someone found us. We were adults. Not a pair of kids getting caught. But if this was someone other than one of our friends, it wouldnt be good, it would be a shit storm. We jumped apart when the door opened, and a grinning Caroline stuck her head in followed by a smirking Brittany.

"Make a run for it BG," Caroline said with a snicker. He gave me another deep kiss before smirking and popping me on the ass making me yelp before strutting to the door. "And Cassie sweetie. May wanna fix that dress. You almost have a nip slip going on."

"Dammit Caroline," I hissed looking down and fixing my dress as they laughed.

"Ladies," Brantley said with a chuckle nodding his head at the girls. "Have a good evening."

"I bet it was for you," Brittany said with a giggle passing me my drink as I walked closer.

"Damn right it was," he murmured with a chuckle winking at me as I blushed. With that he turned and headed out the door down the hall. Caroline leaned her head out checking his ass out as he walked.

"Dammit sister," she said after letting out a low whistle. "Still don't see why your stupid ass won't marry that man."

"Ughhh Caroline dont start tonight please," I whined stumbling a little on my still weak legs as we walked.

"Trouble walking there Cass?" Brittany asked with a laugh.

"Hell yes," I whispered yelled as we walked. "You would too if you if that man had had his hands on you."

"Well of course," Caroline snickered. "That man has a big dick attitude."

"I'll never tell," I said with a wink.

Cure For The Sniffles

December 2015

Cassie's POV

I buried further under the fuzzy blanket I had over me on the couch. I couldnt get warm despite the blanket, fleece leggings, thick socks, and hoodie I had on. I was supposed to be finishing up my Christmas shopping, not huddled on my couch sick as a dog. But yet here I was with the flu a week and a half before Christmas.

I was beyond the point of exhausted but hadn't able to sleep because of coughing. My aunt had finally drug me out of bed this morning to the doctors office. Fussing at me the whole drive for letting myself getting this run down. I knew I needed to get up and find something to eat but just didnt have the energy. I needed to find it before Aunt Shelia got back and read me the riot act. We had already gone one round this morning because the doctor had wanted to admit me and I wasn't having it.

I heard the front door open and moaned at the footsteps. A moment later the blanket was tugged off my face and I blinked my bleary eyes open to see Ben leaning over me with a concerned look on his face.

"Go away Ben," I croaked before another round of coughing started.

"You look like shit Cassie," he said shaking his head and handing me a bottle of water. I flipped him off as he snickered leaning over to kiss my forehead. "Yep, still running fever. Don't move."

"Where would I go dumbass?" I rasped out grabbing my throat from the effort of talking. I burrowed back under my blanket. I had almost fallen asleep when Ben walked back in front of me. My eyes narrowed at the duffle bag in one hand and a pair of my Uggs in the other.

"Come on honey," he said giving me a soft smile pulling me upright and slipping my boots on. "Geez Cass you are shivering."

"I feel like hell Bennie Boo," I muttered wrapping my blanket around me. He tugged my hand pulling me up and wrapped an arm around me. I tucked my phone into my pocket and shuffled along with him as he locked my house up and helped me in the truck. "Where are you taking me?"

"You'll see," Ben murmured with a laugh as he backed out of my driveway. "Try to get some rest on the way."

I stretched out laying my tired head on the console and was asleep before we ever got out of Athens. I vaguely heard my door open before I felt myself being lifted. I was too tired to care right now. I felt Ben's chest rumble under my shoulder as he talked to somebody and my hair being smoothed off my forehead before he started walking again. I was laid down on a soft bed then Ben tugged my boots off before covering me up. I slipped into a deep sleep moments later in the darkened room.

I stirred a few hours later when I felt an arm tighten around my waist and I snuggled closer for warmth. Great if I was still shivering means my damn fever hadn't broke. I opened an eye glancing down at the familiar covers and the tattooed around wrapped around me. I instantly felt guilty.

Brantley was in the middle of a few off weeks before getting back on the road for The Black Out Tour. I didn't need to be getting him sick.

"B..." I groaned and felt a kiss placed to the back of my head. "The last thing you need is to be sick."

"Well darlin," he mumbled as I turned over to face him realizing how pale and tired he looked. "Kinda hard to catch what you already have."

"You have the flu too?" I asked lifting my hand that felt like it weighed a thousand pounds to touch his warm forehead.

"Yes mam," he mumbled with a sigh then crack a bleary eye open to glare at me. "At least mine isn't two steps away from being pneumonia like someone else because they won't slow down and rest."

"Like you have any room to talk," I snapped before having to sit up quickly as I broke out into a coughing fit holding my aching head. I reached back to push his chest weakly. "You're not any better at it than I am."

"Now just a damn minute Cassie," he growled sitting up slowly to glare at me.

"Brantley Keith. Cassandra Nicole," we heard snapped from the doorway. We stopped glaring at each other to turn and see Mama Becky walking in with both hands on her hips. "Both of are need to shut it up right now. Last thing either of you needs is to be wasting energy arguing."

"Yes Mama," we both murmured looking at each other hanging our heads. She walked over sitting on the edge of the big bed feeling both of our foreheads like we were five instead of twenty-seven and thirty. She sighed then pointed a finger at both of us making us hang our heads in shame.

"If I haven't told each of you once, I've told you a hundred times," Mama Becky said glaring at us. "You need to slow down some. Both of you are burning the candles at both ends. And yes before you even waste your breath Brantley Keith, I haven't forgot that you are going into the studio this year. Nor have I forgotten Cass your year is booked as well. Good heavens kids, no wonder you can't make this work. You barely have anytime for yourselves let alone each other. Now, I'm off my soap box. Medicine for both of you then go back to sleep."

"But Mama," Brantley whined pulling me in front of him and sitting his chin on my shoulder. "That shit is so damn nasty. Plus, it knocks my ass out."

"Good," she said smirking at us and handing the medicine over. "You need to sleep grouchy ass. Good thing it kicked in earlier after you heard me talking to Shelia about Cassie being sick. Or I would have had to have hidden all of your keys to keep you from going to Athens. Which is why I called Ben to go get her. I knew she wasn't doing any better than you. Plus, you know you both rest easier if you are together."

We both took the cough syrup she handed us, shuddering then she stood up making her way to the door.

"I've got an errand or two to run," Mama Becky said narrowing her eyes at us. Brantley let out a big sigh then stretched back out tugging me down with him. Sylo came running into the room and curled up with his head at my feet. "I expect you both to get some rest. I may can promise a bowl of chicken and dumplings later. Both of your phones are downstairs with Ben and Kolby. If you need something yell for one of them."

"Awww come on Mama," Brantley muttered getting comfortable as I snuggled into his side my eyes getting heavy. "You are leaving Dumb and Dumber to baby sit us."

"They'd let us die for kicks," I growled.

"Trust me," she said with a grin." I bribed them well. You two will be paying up. That's for sure. Now get some sleep."

A couple weeks later I was sitting with my knees pulled up to my chest with my chin propped on them staring into the blazing fire in front of me. I smiled softly when I felt a pair of arms settle around me and a soft kiss placed on my shoulder where my red sweater had slipped.

Brantley and I both had been still worn down from being sick so we both had turned down a multitude of offers on what to do for New Year's Eve. Kelsey had tried to get me to come to a huge party in L.A. and Luke had begged for both of us to come to a bonfire he was throwing.

"You sure staying in is what you want to do baby?" he murmured pulling me further into this chest and kissing my cheek.

"Yes," I said turning to give him a soft smile as I settled closer and threaded my fingers through his. "You know, I've enjoyed the quiet the last few weeks."

"Me too," Brantley said with a sigh stretching a leg out. "Think we both needed this down time, even if it wasn't all fun and games."

"I agree," I said with a giggle turning to kiss his cheek. He reached up to cup my cheek and leaned down brushing his lips against mine.

"Cass," he said, and I stopped him with a shake of my head.

"Don't Brantley, please," I said giving him a look. "Can we just enjoy ringing in the new year with trying to figure out what is what. I know we have an impossible year ahead of us. How about this? I propose we take what time we can this year. Then later on in the year before we get to wrapped up in whats next we sit down, and figure out us."

"Alright, "he said giving me a soft smile. "But, we are going to make more time for each other this year. I'm fine with keeping it quiet but we need each other baby."

"I know we do," I said quietly looking down at our interlocked fingers." I can do that. Before the end of the year, I agree we figure something out on way or the other."

One Hell of An Amen

November 2016

Cassie's POV

I took a deep breath as the limo moved through the streets of Nashville tapping my nails on my leg as we got closer to the venue for the movie premiere. I had never been more nervous in my life. Granted it wasn't the first one that I had attended over the years but this one meant the most.

I had always been active in what I could involving anything for veterans because of my dad and my grandfather. That involvement had gotten even deeper since I had met Brantley. Even though a few things in the last few years he'd had his hand in, I had been in the background. So, when the script titled One Hell of An Amen was given to me last year I had immediately called Marsha and told her I wanted the role of Stephanie.

The writer and director had been blown away with my audition for the young war widow that they had shut down casting after my audition. They also confessed that some of the decision came from the fact I had a history with the songwriter of the song, but that it had just made them want me for the role more. As a result, half of country music would be in attendance tonight with Brantley, Luke, Jason, FGL and others having contributed to the soundtrack.

I had made mention to Brantley that we could do the carpet together only to get shot down with a soft smile. He would be there every step of the way, just didnt want the sight of us together to take away from my night. Even though I was a little hurt, I couldn't argue the fact with him.

All eyes would be on us anyhow with both of us being there. Marsha reached over to stop my finger from tapping as we pulled up to the theatre. I was nervous because this one meant so much. I could never do another movie again and this would still be my favorite.

"We're here," Marsha said giving me a wide smile and sliding over to get the door. I took a deep breathe, prayed I didn't trip and calmly slid a foot out and accepted the hand of the man opening the door. I waved at the crowd stopping to take a couple of photos and sign autographs. Josh, my co-star from our show had signed on to play my Army Ranger husband in the movie so it had really made it so much easier to film.

He paused to take a couple of photos with me and leaned over to kiss me on the cheek. I could feel the eyes on me but not much I could do. If the tabloids weren't speculating about Brantley and I, they were on a kick about me and Josh. We were nothing more than close friends and B knew it. I made it the end seeing Jason and Luke both doing interviews as Caroline and Brittany spotted me.

They both walked over to hug me as a couple of photographers yelled for us to snap a few photos. It was well known between all three of our social media that we were close friends. I stood in the middle of two of my favorite blondes and pasted a big smile on my face. I swear other than Kate, I was the only dark haired one of the bunch. I knew my cheeks were going to be hurting be the end of the night.

"Oohh sweetie," Caroline hissed under her breath. "If you could just see the undress me eyes you are getting doll."

I briefly turned my head as Brittany giggled and held in an eye roll.

"Like you can see anything with those damn dark sunglasses he's got on," I replied. "Never goes to one of these without them. Keeps them from seeing how many times he rolls his eyes at dumbass questions."

"Oh, please honey," Brittany said giving my side a squeeze as we turned. "We all know that you are getting them."

"Ladies," I said with a wide grin batting my eyes at them as we moved around. "I'm not crazy. I can feel them. Why the hell do you think I picked this dress out."

"Gonna be lucky if he doesn't find a dark room to pin you to the wall in before this ever starts, "Caroline said with a laugh making me crack up. "Be the ACM's all over again."

"Hush your mouth Caroline," I hissed as she grinned at me. I took a look down the carpet where Brantley was being interviewed taking in the dark jeans, tux jacket, boots, and grey button up shirt with the collar opened.

Then that damned hat backwards. He had sent me a selfie earlier when I had been finished getting ready and my jaw had almost dropped. Then I had to stop myself from typing out a text for him to get his ass over here for a quickie before hand. "Although, he knows what that damn hat does to me. I may be the one pinning him to the wall."

Brittany reached a manicured finger up as we reached the doorway and smirked at me as she flicked the black and white diamond ear rings I was wearing tonight. I had teared up when PJ had dropped them off to me earlier with a card and a big smile. It wasn't lost on me that they matched the ring hidden around my neck perfectly.

'Those are gorgeous Cass," she said giving me a knowing smile. "Really complements the dress. But don't think it's lost on either of us they match a certain ring that shall not be named."

"Yea, I know," I said with smile biting my red painted lips. "He sent them to me earlier."

"Cassie," Caroline said crossing her arms giving me a look. "You know it's almost the end of the year. When are you going to give in and marry that man? I need babies to spoil!"

"Well....' I drawled giving her a wink. I did agree to go with him to the CMA's next week. That's a step in the right direction right?"

"A baby step," Caroline growls narrowing her eyes at me tapping a high heel impatiently. "I need giant ones, huge ones, if I ever am going to get babies to spoil. All of mine are growing up!"

"Good lord," I huffed rolling my eyes. "You are starting to sound just like my Aunt Shelia and Mama Becky."I looked up and saw Luke and Jason making their way over to us.

"Luke....." I whined putting my hands on my hips making him laugh. "Make her stop!"

"Pfttt...." Caroline said sticking her tongue out at me. "Like he could."

I went to argue with her but was stopped by Marsha placing a gentle hand on my arm as she gave them all a smile.

"Cassie," she said pointing over to a group of reporters talking to Josh." I need you over there."

"Ok," I said quietly. "I'll see y'all inside."

A little while later I settled into my seat in the middle of the theatre. I was glad they had seated all of us here instead of the very front. I was already uncomfortable in a fancy dress and heels, didn't want to add neck strain to that. I was so damn nervous it wasnt even funny.

Caroline reached over to squeeze my hand as the house lights lowered and the film was getting started. Lauren leaned over my seat kissing my cheek as Thomas kissed the top of my head. She had texted me earlier they were running late and going to sneak in the back.

I really wanted Brantley right now, but I wasn't sure where he was at. I kept bouncing my leg up and down nervously making Luke snicker on the other side of Caroline. I discreetly flipped him off. Marsha glanced over giving me a sympathetic look because she knew I always got like this and never liked to watch myself on screen. She pointed towards the back as she quietly got up heading to the aisle.

I settled in and focused on the screen wringing my hands together. I felt someone settle into the seat beside a few minutes later. I assumed Marsha had made it back so I jumped when I felt a warm hand on my knee that was still bouncing up and down. I let out a gasp then a sigh of relief when I looked over to see Brantley sitting next to me. He laced our fingers together then leaned over to kiss my cheek.

"Calm down Cass," he whispered before kissing my cheek. "You know the audience is going to love it. I have complete faith you knocked it out of the park."

I calmly nodded my head and settled it against his shoulder. Amazing at how quick just a touch from him could calm the nerves down. I lifted my head looking at him as he gave me a grin.

"Thanks B," I whispered. "That's what I needed. I needed to hear that from you."

A while later I walked into the private after party that Luke had arranged. Other than a few outside snapping photos of people going in, he had been adamant that no press was allowed. PJ had been waiting on me when I got to the car to bring me over with a wide smile and a big hug before he helped me in.

Kept raving about how damn good the movie was. I followed Caroline inside and headed straight for the wooden bar at the back kicking my shoes off and leaning down to pick them up. I heard a laugh and looked up to see Tyler dangling a shot in front of me with a wide grin. I gave him one back and tossed it back before standing on tip toe to kiss his cheek.

"Thanks, THubb," I said then leaned over to tackle Hailey with a hug. "You don't know how much I needed that."

"Oh, I can just imagine honey," Tyler said with a laugh as I made my way over to sit down. "You did an amazing job."

Caroline took a foot to slide the stool next to her out for me and passed me another shot. She saluted me as I sat down and we both tossed them back. Luke leaned around her as I got settled trying to get comfortable on this stool in this dress.

"You did an amazing job sweetheart," he said giving me his trademark grin.

"Yes, she did," I heard murmured behind me as I felt warmth at my back and a familiar pair of hands landed on my shoulders squeezing gently.

I sighed and leaned back into Brantley's chest soaking in the warmth letting it calm my nerves at what they all were going to really think.

"Thanks guys," I said quietly giving them a smile as he wrapped an arm around my waist then took the bottle of water Tyler handed him as Hailey settled in beside me. "I just hope I did it justice. This one meant more to me than anything I have ever done."

"I won't lie," Hailey said squeezing my hand and giving me a wink. "I cried. Even had to pass a tissue over to Tyler. The damn funeral scene near about killed me."

"Lord yes it did," Jason said from the other side of Brantley leaning down to pass me a beer. "I jumped right along with you on each shot of the twenty-one-gun salute."

"Then that acoustic version of the song Brantley," Caroline said giving him a smile. "Sent chills down my spine buddy. I haven't heard your voice sound that pure in years."

Thank you darlin," he said leaning over to give her a kiss on the cheek. "They did a hell of a job on song choices for the sound track for sure."

"Thanks, y'all," I said tucking my head down and blushing as I received a few more compliments. "Means more to me coming for y'all than any review."

"Darlin," Brantley said looking down at me smiling. "Only you could have made this movie what it was. So damn real. Anyone else, well..hell it just wouldn't have worked."

"Well," Brian Davis said walking up and shouldering Jason out of the way to hug me and kiss my cheek. He gave me a big wink before putting a hand on Brantley's shoulder. "It helped that she was around when that song was written. May have had her nose buried in scripts but she saw it all happen. She knew what it meant and still does."

"Thanks Brian," I said smiling at him before taking a sip feeling myself finally relax. To hell with what the reviews said. I had heard all I needed to hear. "You know that songs a special place for me because of my family. If they had given it to any other actress. Well I would have pitched a bitch fit that all of Hollywood would still be talking about. Would have showed them just how mad a real Southern Belle can get."

"Of that I have no doubt," Caroline said with a laugh. She clapped her hands together as the music cranked up. "Now, that's my jam and I need to shake it. Luke's not that only one who can you know. I taught him all he knows! Come on Cass!"

She grabbed my hand and tugged me and Brittany out onto the dance floor as the rest of the girls followed suit. Typical Luke, he couldn't stand it and joined us a minute later. A while later I was laughing and out of breath from dancing as the DJ slowed it down. A soft smile grazed my lips as I recognized the melody. Damn, I hadn't heard "Amazed" in years. A second later a felt a hand on my back and Brantley spun me around to wrap his arms around me pulling me closer. Caroline winked at me as she walked off the dance floor to go find Luke.

"Well someone remembers the first song we ever dance too, Brantley said with a quiet laugh leaning his forehead against mine. "I know it's one I will never forget. Changed my life that night and I'd like to think it changed yours."

"Lord did it," I said softly and placed a gentle kiss on his lips. I wrapped my arms around his neck getting closer. Damn, the smell of his cologne was driving me crazy. "Still think about it every time I am headed back to Athens from your Mama's. Here stood this man who was supposed to be a cocky bad ass and was giving me a shy smile in the back of a truck bed on a starry night out at Potts asking me to dance. Fell a little bit in love with you that night."

"Darlin," Brantley said lifting his head and cupping my cheek as we swayed to the music. "I fell head over heels in love with you the first time I saw you at that show you came to see Ben at. You made me forget all about booze and or the need to take a pill. I was just content to spend time with you. You knocked my right off my feet with a smile." He leaned down to kiss me. "Wish I had gotten my act together a lot sooner baby."

"Babe," I said lifting a hand to his cheek stroking his bearded cheek. "Well, it all worked out didn't it."

"Yea," he said sighing giving me a knowing look. "It did. But not completely. I don't have you locked in with ring on a very important finger. Not yet anyhow."

"B...." I said making him chuckle just a little. I buried my head into his shoulder as he rubbed a hand down my back. The ring around my neck felt like it burned with that one still unanswered question. He had broached the subject, argued with me, begged, and I still put him off.

"I know," I grumbled closing my eyes just enjoying the feel of his arms around me." I know."

"One day baby girl," he whispered leaning down to kiss my neck. "One day very soon you are going to give in and quit fighting me. But that's not what tonight is about. Tonight is about celebrating the kick ass movie you did baby."

No Comment

February 2017

Brantley's POV

I buried my face into Cassie's neck pressing my bare chest to her back as she tried to tug a shirt over her head.

"Brantley," she giggled making me laugh. "Stop that tickles and you know it."I wrapped my arms around her tighter sliding my hands up and down her bare stomach trying to get to the button of her jeans but all I got was her smacking my hand away making me sigh. I wanted nothing more than to get her back in that bed where we had been since she pounced on me after soundcheck.

She finally had put her foot down with Marsha that her schedule needed to match mine as much in off time as it could. That and she wanted to be able to come out to as many shows as she could this year. "You know you have to leave for VIP in five minutes so stop."

"Fine," I grumbled popping her on the ass as she let out a yelp pushing my shoulder. I caught the shirt she tossed me in midair and slipped it over my head just as I heard a knock on the bus door. I grabbed my hat off the bed flipping it around backwards giving her a wide smirk as she slipped her boots on and I held a hand out to her. We walked hand in hand to the front of the bus to walk out and see a grinning PJ waiting with the golf cart. I helped Cassie climb on before settling in behind her.

"For someone who was so sick last week," PJ said giving her a grin and a wink. "Someone finally looks more rested."

"Yea well," she said turning her head to wink at me. She had quickly braided her hair when we had gotten out of the shower fifteen minutes ago. "That one back there makes me rest any chance he gets."

"Damn right," I murmured leaning forward to kiss her cheek as we pulled up outside the tent. Cassie picked up the hat PJ'd had for her and tugged it over her eyes. "You will work yourself the bone if not."

We made our way inside as Cassie moved to hide in the back with PJ as I grabbed my guitar to head on the small stage with Jesse. I kept my eyes on the back when we played "My Kinda Crazy". I could see the soft smile on Cass's face. She loved that song. I sat my guitar to the side and opened up the questioning. It was a few kids here tonight, so they should keep it fairly tame.

I had to smother a grimace when the age old question of whether I was single or not came up. If people just knew how tired of answering this question, from every fan, member of the press to my own Mama, I was tired of not having the answer I wanted so I decided to be a smart ass tonight. I was beyond sick of not having the woman I loved the way I wanted her.

"Well darlin," I said rubbing my chin and pasting a wide smirk on my face as I cut my eyes to the back meeting a glaring pair of chocolate brown ones. "You want the official or unofficial answer to that."

I gave the young girl a wink the picked another question to change the subject. I saw a blur of red long sleeve t-shirt as Cassie stalked out the back. Yay, I thought with a sigh before focusing back on the group. Getting back on the bus after this was gonna be so much fun.

I wrapped things up then headed to find PJ shaking his head at me as I took off to the bus with a jog knowing that I just needed to get this argument over with. I keyed in the code and stepped on the quiet bus to find a snarling Cassie standing in the middle of the lounge glaring at me.

"What the hell were you thinking Brantley?" she snapped. Her cheeks were still so pale from being sick last week that the flush from her being pissed almost matched her shirt.

"Well I didn't answer, did I?" I drawled giving her a wink. I ducked the remote that whizzed by my head and stalked forward to the refrigerator to grab a bottle of water.

"You insinuated that something was going on jackass," she growled tapping her foot on the floor in irritation. "Really B, unofficial or official version!"

"Well...." I said turning my head giving her a look as I opened the water. "Technically baby, they just asked if I was single." I stopped mid chug of water when a Nike I had left laying around earlier nailed me in the back.

"You know that there is no way you are single," Cassie said putting her hands on her hips glaring at me as I turned to meet her glare." If you so much as whisper you are I will beat your ass Brantley Keith!"

I stalked toward her with my shoulders thrown back making Cassie gasp then take a step back as I leaned down to glare at her. She had gotten me good and pissed now. I was tired of having this argument. I was just so fucking tired! But dammit, I wasn't going to let her go.

"Well then," I seethed making her eyes widen a little. "Take the fucking ring off the damn chain Cassandra Nicole. That will solve the damn problem. Quit hiding behind work and marry me! Haven't we proved the last six months we can juggle things a little better."

I brushed past her stalking off the bus. I paused at the bottom of the steps lighting a cigarette as I heard her frustrated yell from inside the bus. I couldn't help the evil grin that spread across my lips as I took a drag. Yea, well welcome to the club sweetheart. I looked over to see PJ leaned against the side shaking his head at me.

"Boss," he said with a sigh. "What did you do now to piss her off?"

"Told her to take the damn ring off the chain around her neck," I grumbled looking around. "That if she didn't want any more questions of if I am single or not. Put the fucker back on her finger where it belongs."

"Oh Boss," he said with wide eyes. "You've done it now."

"She'll get over it," I said shrugging my shoulders pushing off the side of the bus. I was about to head towards the venue when his voice stopped me.

"No man," he said trying to keep a laugh in. "You've really gone and done it now."

"Huh?" I asked in confusion before I felt a hard smack across my ass making me yelp and jump. I spun around to see a glaring Cassie holding a big wooden spoon in her hand with an evil grin spread across her lips. I glared right back at her rubbing my ass cheek. Only my Mama would think to stock my buss with one of those just for that. I stomped over to her glaring.

"Cassie," I growled crossing my arms over my chest. "That fucking hurt."

"Yes B. I am sure it did," she snarked back meeting my glare with a raised eyebrow. "You know you deserved it."

"Well," I grumbled. "I'm tired of the same old answer."

"We have talked about this Brantley," she said throwing her hands up in the frustration pausing to cough since her throat was still scratchy. "It just complicates things when the whole world knows. We get a little bit of peace this way."

"No dammit!" I snapped shaking my head. "Cassie, you have talked, and I have listened. Oh, baby have I. I have done what you wanted because I know that if I don't I risk the chance of losing you all over again. I can't go there again baby. We were miserable without each other. But how is this limbo any better! I am just so damn tired of it all!"

I turned on my heel and stalked off not looking back as I marched my way into the venue.

Cassie's POV

"B!" I yelled out after him stomping my foot but he never checked up and I lost sight of him. I leaned against the bus with a heavy sigh. "Dammit."

"Man's got a point," PJ said moving to mirror my pose and looking down at me.

"Don't you start too PJ," I growled blinking back tears. I hated fighting with him. Especially when I had such a damn busy next two weeks it would be after that before I saw him again.

"Oh yes I will," he growled back leveling me with a stare. I could see the concern there. I saw it from all the guys here lately. Ben and Brantley especially. "You need to slow down Cassie. Honey, it's the end of February and youve already been sick once. Every time this bus rolls out and youre not on it or flying to see him, he worries. I've never seen a pair more destined to be together but spend so much time apart."

"PJ," I sniffled quietly. "I don't know if I can slow down. Every time I think about it, something else comes up."

"It's called saying no sweetheart," he said laying a big hand on my shoulder giving it a gentle squeeze. He gave me a knowing look. I knew he knew how busy I stayed. If Brantley was home, he had taken to traveling with me some if I needed the security. Wasn't anyone I trusted more other than B or Ben to keep me safe. "The most I have seen you relax in the last year is when he makes you."

"Ughhhh....." I groaned making him chuckle as I pushed a loose strand of hair out of my face. "I hate when you are right PJ. But knowing it and being able to do it is my problem."

"Well honey," PJ said with a smirk. "You need to remember who works for you. Tell them no like you tell Boss no. Start standing up for yourself. It's your life. Your career, not anyone else's. Because mark my words on this honey, if you end up in the hospital due to exhaustion, and sweetheart if you keep this pace up, it's coming. You won't have seen caveman like you will then. That man will not give a fuck who is around. And then what you try to keep as a precious guarded secret will be well known. He will only have one thought and that will be to get to you. Everyone else standing in his way be damned."

"He has been more vocal about it lately," I muttered biting my lip. "PJ, I'm just so damn afraid of losing him."

"Cass, y'all have been in this boat for how long," PJ said shaking his head. "He's still here. Yea, he got aggravated and frustrated tonight sure. I don't think you realize sometimes just how much that man loves you. It's really past time you put you and him first."

"I know," I sighed then looked over at him. "We matched the first half of the year up pretty okay. But I have turned down any more parts for the rest of the year and next. Told Marsha that I was taking a break and some time for myself."

"Really?" he asked with wide eyes and a big grin spread across his face. "Finally, darlin."

"Yea well," I said with a half-smile. "With the show ending, I'm free and clear for a while after May other than a few interviews that I am sure will come up. So, looks like y'all will have me tagging along on the summer leg of the tour. Unless he's still pissed at me. But dammit PJ, don't tell him. Please. I'm trying to figure out how."

He pointed at the golf cart then held out a hand helping me climb on before moving around to the driver's seat. He smirked at me as he took off towards the venue.

"Well....." he drawled with a laugh. "I can think of a good way."

"What's that PJ?" I said as I typed out a text to Brantley that I was sorry.

"Take the damn ring off your neck," he said with a smirk. "Put it where it belongs."

"Dammit PJ," I huffed rolling my eyes. "Not you too."

He let out deep laugh throwing his head back as he parked and walked around to help me out. I gave his big shoulder a push as we walked into the venue.

"Well you wanted to know how," he said grinning down at me as we walked. "That is as good as way as any. Besides, you know you want to."

I glared up at him then rolled my eyes. "I hate it when either of you are right, "I grumbled.

"Well, "PJ said with a laugh as we made our way to the back-stage area. "If you drag your feet any longer missy, hes gonna hog tie you and put it there himself. He's so aggravated now, he'd liable to do it live."

I paused as I felt myself grow pale making PJ spin around to look at me with concern. I narrowed my eyes and pointed a finger at him.

"He wouldn't dare," I muttered shaking my head. "He knows how I feel. Besides it may back fire on him."

"Oh yes he would!" PJ said cracking up. "He's about done resolved himself that will be the only way. If he backs you into a corner."

"Fuck PJ!" I yelled covering my eyes. This was so not my night right now. "He can't do that. I told him to give me this year to figure this out and I am working on it. I really am."

PJ walked over draping a big arm over my shoulders guiding me to the backstage area.

"Cass," he rumbled with a quiet chuckle. "That was for 2016 sweetie. In case you haven't noticed, it's 2017. See, been so damn busy you forgot your year agreement was up. Way he sees it, now all bets are off sugar."

"Shit," I yelped looking up at him. "Fucking hell PJ! Please, please, tell me his isn't planning anything with this rowdy ass crowd tonight!"

PJ gave me a wide cheesy grin the pushed me towards where the guys were standing in a circle getting ready to do their pre-concert prayer.

"Never know about Boss," he whispered in my ear as I glared at him as I walked over to Brantley. I wrapped my arm around his waist as he tucked me into his side as I bowed my head. He squeezed me closer and kissed to top of my head. I glanced up at him under my lashes and he was watching me closely.

I narrowed my eyes at the twinkle in his and I knew my ass was in trouble. Jesse closed the prayer and the guys headed to take their places on stage. Brantley took his mic and adjusted his ear monitors before wrapping me up in his arms kissing me deeply. He pulled back rubbing his hand on my back and giving me a wink.

"Love you baby girl," he murmured.

"Love you too," I said as he turned to jog on stage. "What are you up to hotshot?"

"Who me?" he called back before disappearing under the stage. I rolled my eyes and wandered over to the stool PJ had sitting to the side for me. I got settled and cheered as Ben hit the first notes for "It's About to Get Dirty". I loved to watch them play live. I had missed so much over the last couple of years.

I felt a wide smile spread across my lips as Brantley took his guitar from a roadie and they started "Outlaw in Me". I loved this one. I let out gasp and PJ laughed beside me as photos of me played on the screen behind the stage. I covered my mouth as tears started to form, especially one that I had realized Mama Becky had snapped this past Christmas of us kissing under the mistletoe.

"See darlin," PJ said with a grin leaning down in my ear. "I told you he wasn't playing fair anymore."

I looked over to see Brantley cutting his eyes over to me a soft smile on his face as he sang. I couldn't help but wipe at the tears on my face. I knew he loved me and understood me like no one else ever could. That man right there was made for me. He knew that I loved him the same way. I wiped at my face leaning forward to hide the tears from him. I've got to get my shit together, I thought sighing and trying to get my emotions under control.

I cant expect that man to wait around forever and to be honest, I was tired of fighting it.

Life Changing Phone Calls

March 2017

Cassie's POV

I dropped the phone in shock and covered my mouth as the person on the other line ended the call. I sank down onto my couch as tears formed in my eyes. No, no, no. Not possible. This had to be a damn joke. Could not be true. I pulled my knees up to my chest as I started to sob.

Fuck! Needless to say, my whole world was just turned upside down with one phone call. What was I going to do? I didn't even know where to start on how to feel about this. Could I even do this? I wasn't sure how long I sat there alternating between tears and panicking. I jumped to my feet when I heard a key hit my front door and boot steps. I didn't even notice that I had been sitting in the dark.

"Cass," I heard mumbled before the light for the living room switched on. I looked up to see Brantley standing there giving me a confused look. "Baby, are you ok? Why have you been crying?"

I completely forgot he was flying back in today. Even though we weren't officially together to the public, we had tried to match our schedules up better when he had planned this tour. I glared at him making him give me a wary eye as he tried to step towards me. I felt the tears start falling more and I reached over to grab the first thing I could find on the coffee table which was the TV remote and tossed it at his head.

"What in the fucking hell has gotten in to you?" he growled ducking his head as I continued to sob. "Geez Cass, is it that time of the month?"

I gasped in a deep breath then launched the book I had been reading the other day at him nailing his shoulder. I knew I looked like a crazy person right now, but I didn't care.

"For fucks sake Cassandra!" Brantley yelled as I glared and moved away any time he tried to get close to me. "I know you're approaching thirty but shit, I thought we had years to worry about you going through the change. Woman, care to explain why you are acting crazy!"

"I'm pregnant you damn moron! Not going through menopause!" I snarled. "Don't ever try to say that I am getting old again!"

He turned pale and collapsed onto the couch. I stood there heaving out sobs as he looked at me with wide eyes. He pulled his hat off tossing it on the coffee table as he ran a big hand over his buzzed hair.

"Cass," Brantley said quietly. "How did this happen? We've always been careful. I was joking a couple of months ago so please don't think I did anything. I know how important your career is honey. Are you sure?"

"Yes," I gasped out wrapping my arms around my waist. "Remember how I came down with strep right after the tour started? Well even though I'm on the shot, apparently antibiotics effect it and we didn't use anything as back up!"

"Fuck," he murmured rubbing his hand over his beard in shock as I stared at him. "Baby, come here."

"No," I growled at him shaking my head. I covered my face and moaned. " Oh God. There's so much gossip about whether I am with you or Josh! Your fans are gonna think I'm such a whore! I'm never going to be able to show my face around Nashville again.

"Sweetheart," he said shaking his head as he stood up to guide me down to the couch wrapping his arms around me. He cupped my chin wiping the tears away with his thumb as I looked up at him with watery eyes. "First of all, ever since the CMA's, the press, fans, everyone, have pretty much figured you are with me. Official statement or not. Not to mention the added pictures of you in my show or the picture you put on Instagram a few weeks ago of us snuggled on the couch on the bus. Can't see my face but the damn tattoo is a dead giveaway. Second, our friends and family know we've barely been apart when we could the last few years. Baby, to hell with what any of the rest of them say."

"I just don't want anyone to think that of me," I sniffled biting my lip.

"Fuck them if they do," Brantley murmured kissing my cheek. "Know damn well I'm the only man you have ever been with."

"Ruined me for all the rest," I snarked making him chuckle as I settled my head against his shoulder. My eyes teared up again as he settled a big hand across my stomach stroking gently. I laid my hand over his linking our fingers. We sat there quietly for a few minutes before he spoke again.

"How'd you find out Cass?" Brantley asked as I lifted my eyes to look at him.

"I had gotten sick the other day on set," I answered making him narrow his eyes at me. Oh boy here we go. "Been tired too. I just thought it was because still worn down from being sick. We've been having issues with getting these last few episodes filmed. So, I went for a check-up and she drew some blood for bloodwork. I got the call earlier right when I got home."

"Baby," he growled. "I know it's down to crunch time on wrapping this season, but you have got to slow down. You can bet your ass that I will make sure of it now. This baby is part of me too and I couldn't handle it if anything happened to either of you. I know, you know."

"Know what?" I asked giving him a puzzled look.

"That you are taking time off after this," Brantley said giving me a look. I closed my eyes and bit my lip. Shit, who spilled the beans I wondered. I had planned on telling him when he got home.

"Who told you?" I asked with a sigh. "PJ or Ben because they were the only two who could have."

"Ben," he said with a laugh. "Let it slip on the flight home. Said he was glad we would have an extra tag along for the summer leg of the tour. When were you going to tell me?"

"Tonight," I sighed playing with the rings on his fingers. "I wasn't sure if you would want me around though after our last fight and then this bombshell was dropped on me."

"Cass," he said shaking his head. I always want you around. "That's why I get so frustrated. I've gotten so little time with you as it is at times. Was this the only change you had been thinking of making? Because Cassie honey, I've only been begging for the last two years."

I could hear the hope in his voice even if he was trying to keep his face blank. PJ was right, as far as Brantley was concerned, all bets were off. The subject had been coming up more and more. He took a finger and hooked it into the chain under my t-shirt pulling it out.

"That's part of the reason I wanted time off," I whispered. "I wanted to talk to you about it. But the news I got today changes things a little doesn't it."

"Get that thought out of your head right now," Brantley growled sitting up wrapping his arms around me. "My wanting to marry you doesn't have a damn thing to do with you being pregnant. That damn ring should have never left your finger to begin with. Should have a wedding band to go along with it now but we let our damn careers get in the way. That's not going to happen this time I can fucking promise you that. We will not lose sight of us again."

"I want that," I said tearing up. Damn hormones. "I'm tired of avoiding the questions knowing my ring is still around my neck and if I have been cornered at the airport this past year, its usually while I am catching a flight to come see you. While I know I've never had to worry about you, Im tired of every fan girl thinking she may have a shot just because there's not a ring on your finger. I'm just so damn tired and have been. I know I need to slow down and well, with the baby, I know I have no choice now. Maybe this is God's way of telling us it's time."

"While its not what I want, I'm not holding you to anything Cass because you are pregnant," he said looking into my eyes and biting his lip.

" I know if I back you into a corner because of it, it will not end well. You can be even more stubborn than me. I will say this, we can make it work. We've proved pretty much the last year we can. I can make my schedule more flexible now than I could and with you taking time off I can shift stuff if I need to even if you are out with us. You and our child are going to come first no matter what."

"You said you would never give up," I said giving him a small smile. "That's the reason this chain has hardly ever left my neck these last few years."

"No baby," he said kissing me gently. "And that fact right there and a promise I made to you and Mama both I would be better, is all that kept me from hitting the bottle after I walked out of this house that night. I knew if I went down that road, no matter how much it hurt right then, I would lose you for good. With that being said, I'm not going to put that ring back on your finger."

"Do what?" I said with wide eyes as he shifted me off his lap and leaned over to kiss me quickly brushing a hand over my stomach before standing up. Brantley picked his hat up off the coffee table slipping it on. "What the fuck is that supposed to mean?"

"What it means Cass," he said looking at me. "You know how I feel. I have made no bones about the fact that I want to marry you. Have wanted to for years. That hasn't and will not change. Me, the man who is afraid of commitment has been hounding your ass off and on for the last two. I'm gonna go because I've got to get Sylo from Mama and maybe we both need a little time to think and process all this a little. Love you. "

With that he kissed my cheek on more time before pulling his keys out of his pocket walking out the door. I was still sitting there in shock when I heard his truck leave a minute later.

"What the hell has gotten into your Daddy? Halfway expected him to hog tie me and toss me on a plane to Vegas as soon as I told him about you," I murmured putting my hand on my stomach.

I paused when I realized what I had done as things got even more real. My stomach flipped with nerves and I started to feel queasy all over again. I got off the couch picking my phone up as I slipped on the shoes I had kicked off earlier before grabbing my purse and keys off the table by the door.

I climbed in my car and with the intent of heading to the store for the Sprite and crackers I had forgotten earlier today. I hummed along with Luke on the radio as I drove. I took a wrong turn and cussed under my breath then pulled into the first parking lot I saw to turn around and back track. My eyes widened when I looked up realizing I had pulled into the lot for the 40 Watt Club.

I smiled thinking about the first time I ever laid eyes on Brantley backstage that night. My heart had literally skipped a beat when had walked over during his set leaning down to sing to me. I may have had some competition for his attention that night, but I hadn't since. I knew without a shadow of a doubt that man was all mine.

I lifted a hand to my lips smiling thinking about that first kiss and the thousands since. I turned the car around to find the street I needed and gasped as "Amazed" started playing through the radio. I gripped the steering wheel as my eyes teared up.

I can still years later see the unsure look in his eyes as he jumped up from leaning against the back of his truck holding a hand down for me asking me to dance the first time that star light night. He had been so unsure and I knew now he had been doing the same thing I had been at the time, trying to hold back. Hearing that, I knew I didn't want to hold back any more. I took the next right and headed out of town.

A little while later I hit the button on my visor to open the big black iron gates and headed up the paved driveway parking on the other side of Brantley's truck. I sat looking at the house and the man I loved so damn much as I reached up to unhook the chain off my neck before sliding my ring back onto my finger. I felt more complete than I had in years.

He was right, it never should have left my finger to begin with. The lights were off except for upstairs. I used my keys to open the front door locking it behind me as sat them down toeing off my shoes. Sylo was sitting at the bottom of the stairs watching me. I paused to place a kiss on his soft head as I scratched his ears.

I gave him one more pat before quietly making my way up the stairs. I could hear the tv playing as I paused at the open bedroom door leaning against it. Brantley was stretched out in bed flipping channels. As if he sensed me, he looked up locking his eyes with mine giving me a smirk.

"I figured you would be over at some point," he said shaking his head as I rolled my eyes and walked over to the closet coming back out a minute later after trading my leggings and t-shirt for one of his to sleep in. "Always got to have your damn snuggles."

"Oh, shut up you ass," I grumbled pulling the covers back as he chuckled holding an arm out for me as I snuggled into his side letting out a sigh. I leaned up giving him a soft kiss then laid my head on his shoulder as I got comfortable. I poked his chest then laid my hand in the middle of his making him laugh. "Like you sleep any better without me."

"Very true baby," he whispered kissing the top of my head and lifting his hand to thread his fingers through mine. He rubbed his thumb over my fingers as he glanced back at the TV.

" I sleep like shit when I don't have you beside me." He stopped a second later as I felt his thumb bump my finger. I waited with baited to see what he would say. Brantley sat up quickly dislodging my head from his shoulder and held my hand up to look at it. He looked down at the ring then at me a couple of times.

I could see the light sheen of tears in his eyes before he swallowed deeply before speaking again. "Baby, are you serious right now? Because honey, if this is a joke I can't handle it."

I sat up placing my free hand on his cheek my own eyes shining with tears.

"I've never been more sure of anything in my life B," I said giving him a watery smile as he let out the shaky breath he had been holding. "You're right, it never should have come off. We should have tried harder. I should have tried harder."

He leaned over to kiss me so hard I lost my breath as he pulled me closer. A second later he broke the kiss and gave me the biggest smile I had seen from him in quite a while.

"Just so you know," he growled playfully pushing me back against the pillows leaning over me to bite my lip gently. "That sucker is not coming off again. You hear me. This it. You are mine. You have always been mine. No take backs, do not pass Go. Better get to planning a wedding woman, because I'm not gonna wait much longer to be able to call you my wife."

"Yes sir," I said giving him a wink wrapping my arms around his neck tugging his lips down to mine. "I want that more than you know."

Finally, Put A Ring On It

Cassie's POV

I braced my hands on the bathroom sink in our hotel suite closing my eyes. I prayed that the wave of nausea would pass. Morning sickness my ass. More like morning, noon, and night. I had taken something for it when I finished my makeup. I breathed in through my nose and out through my mouth. Please, please don't let me puke on the red carpet tonight. I heard the bathroom door open and a second later a big hand slid across my stomach rubbing gently.

"You okay baby?" Brantley asked as I opened my eyes to meet his concerned ones in the mirror. "Anything I can do?"

"No," I moaned leaning back against his chest. "I took my medicine earlier. It should be working soon. Please, please, tell me that we have aisle seats."

He chuckled turning me around to lift my left hand up placing a soft kiss on my ring finger. He'd had to go to interviews earlier in the day so I knew that he would know. We had kept it quiet from everyone that I would be here tonight. I had slept until he had gotten back. I couldn't wait to see the look on Caroline's face.

I had finished the few scenes I had to film yesterday morning then went for my first OB appointment that afternoon. She confirmed that I was about six weeks along based from my blood work. Brantley had been worried because I had been sick. She assured him to make sure I ate small meals and kept hydrated.

"Yes baby," he said kissing my forehead. "We are on the aisle. But hopefully you will be ok. Be a dead giveaway if you took off running in the middle of the show."

"Not funny," I groaned glaring at him before pushing his chest weakly as I walked out to get my clutch. B walked out checking his phone then walked over holding a hand out to me.

"Ready to go?" he said lacing our fingers together then opening the door. We made our way to the elevator. I laid my head on his chest as we rode it down then headed out to the SUV where Rich was waiting on us. Brantley helped me in before climbing in shutting the door. He pulled me close as the we moved through traffic towards the awards venue. Rich turned in the front seat looking at us.

"Congratulations again to both of you," he said with a big grin. "How you want to handle this BG?"

"Oh, I dunno," Brantley said with a wide smile looking down at me. "I think just let the ring do the talking and go from there. I think they will all be ecstatic to get an answer and not hear no comment."

"Alright," Rich said with a chuckle as I rolled my eyes.

"I forgot something," Brantley murmured leaning down to whisper in my ear making me shiver. "I forgot to tell you how beautiful you look tonight baby."

"Thank you," I said leaning up to kiss him softly then wiping away the pink lipstick with my thumb. "Looking pretty good yourself hotshot."

I took a deep breath as the vehicle stopped. Brantley kissed my cheek then placed his hand on the door. I nodded my head letting him know I was ready to go. He opened the door stepping out then turned back holding a hand out to help me. I slid over the leather seat then slowly placed a heeled foot on the ground as I stepped out never taking my eyes off of his. I could see the flashes and hear the cheers around us.

He wrapped an arm around my waist as we walked part way down the carpet then stopped. Brantley gave me a wink then tugged me closer bending me slightly over his arm kissing me deeply. I draped my left hand on his shoulder gripping his jacket. I knew my ring was on perfect display. I heard a loud scream making us break apart. Brantley looked back behind us and started laughing.

"Well," he murmured helping me stand back up. "Someone is a little excited. She almost run Luke over trying to get by him."

I turned to see Caroline barreling down on us as fast as her high heels would let her. Brittany turned her head narrowing her eyes our way as Caroline went past her. I calmly held my left hand up for her to see with a smile. She tugged out of Jason's arms so fast mid pose for photos that he almost fell over. To say were causing a spectacle on the red carpet was putting it nicely. They both reached us and tackled me. Brantley holding me up was the only thing keeping the three of us from hitting the ground in a pile of dresses and heels.

"What the hell do you mean sporting that rock on this red carpet and not giving me a heads up?" Caroline said pulling back to glare at me. I gave her a sheepish grin. "I didn't even know you were coming."

"Surprise," I said with a laugh as she pushed my shoulder lightly making Brantley's hand tighten on my hip slightly. Oh me, he was going to be overprotective. I already knew it. We had both agree to wait until I was further along to tell anyone about the baby. Mama, bless her soul, had started hinting about grandbabies as soon as walked into her kitchen the other day wearing my ring.

"You have got some explainin to do heifer," Brittany said shaking a finger at me. I noticed she looked a little paler than normal. Must be the camera flashes. She reached over to poke Brantley in the chest. "Don't think you are off the hook either buster. I would have bet good money everyone in the whole world would have been able to hear the yell from you when you got her to say yes again."

He smirked over at both of them turning me in front of him, so I could lean against his chest. I was thankful because I was feeling a little woozy. I felt him shrug his shoulders as I placed my hands on top of his. Well, the press usually wanted a photo op, they were getting one and neither of us could give two shits less right now.

"We talked about it," Brantley said. "But since this just happened this past weekend, we decided to let her surprise y'all on the carpet and let the ring do the talking."

"Thank you, Jesus," Caroline said looking up at the darkening desert sky then back at me with a wide grin. "It was about damn time."

"What the hell is going on?" Luke asked walking over to us. He gave B a quick bro hug then kissed my cheek.

"Y'all do realize this is the red carpet," Jason said shaking his head with a grin as Brittany elbowed him in the side. I held my hand up giving them both a wink as I heard someone else call out.

"What the hell y'all!" I heard turning to see Thomas and Lauren making their way over. "You're holding up traffic! We are in Vegas not Georgia!"

"Yes! YES!!!" Lauren squealed dropping his hand and darting over to me.

"Lauren," Brantley grumbled catching her arm as her foot caught right before she got to us. He helped her stand back up straight. "You have got to be careful. Little miss is getting all shook up."

"I know," she said putting a hand on her baby bump. "Got a little excited. Finally. I am so glad you come to your senses Cassie."

"Hey!" I growled shaking my head. "Why has it got to be me? Being with him is not a cakewalk you know."

"Please girl," Thomas said wrapping an arm around his wife and grinning at me.

"Exactly," Jason said with a loud laugh. "We all know it was you dragging your feet. I was worried that my kids would be having kids before you two got your shit together."

"Well," Luke said with a wide grin looking at his watch. "Duty calls. I've got to go get ready. But we are gonna celebrate so damn hard when this is over."

"Damn right," Thomas said with a laugh. "To hell with the awards. BG is the ultimate winner tonight. Congrats to both of you."

We were all motioned to head inside. Brantley held an arm out for me and the other for Caroline to hang on to. Man knew by now that no matter how much experience we had with these, walking in these heels were a bitch. I'd had three pair vetoed when picking out a last minute dress because he thought they were too high. I had reminded him that they would be coming off the first chance I got and he knew it. We paused in the lobby of the venue to talk before heading to our seats.

"Ok," Brittany asked with a smile. " I got to ask, did he top the ornament idea this time?"

"Yes," Caroline said with an equally wide smile. I swear she was like a kid in a candy store. "I need details. I know after all this time you came up with something good BG."

"Nope," Brantley said with a wink. "I had actually quit asking. She put it back on all by herself."

They both looked at each other then over at me as Lauren laughed.

"What you two?" Lauren said with a smile and a wink at Brantley. "She's a smart woman. We know that. Cass, I just didn't know it would take him quitting asking for you to finally cave. Trust me, when you get ready to start a family, and I doubt you two are gonna wait, it will put a lot of things into perspective."

I paled slightly as Brantley's arm tightened around me. Caroline narrowed her eyes at my reaction but didn't say anything. Hope Brittany didn't think it went unnoticed about the look she and Jason snuck at each other at her words.

"Yep," I said clearing my throat. "Taking some time off for a while so I can travel with him. That will be discussed I am sure."

"Sooo..." Thomas said with a smile pointing a finger back and forth between us. "We are in Vegas. BG we need to take our after party to a chapel so you can get her locked down."

"Nah man," Brantley said with a deep laugh. "Though she is surprised I didn't suggest it as soon as I found the ring back on her finger. But I told her she better get to planning something soon though. We've both waited long enough."

"Any ideas?" Caroline asked. "I can come down to the set next week and help you start some planning."

"I've been looking," I said with a smile. "We don't want anything big so June or July is looking good. Been looking at everyone's schedules trying to find a date that would match up. So keep that in mind boys when y'all start planning stuff to do in your off time then."

Secrets Uncovered

C assie's POV

I bit the inside of my cheek as a wave of nausea rolled through my stomach. We were standing by the outdoor pool of what was thankfully our hotel for one of the after parties. I kept the smile on my face as someone stopped to offer us congratulations. I had thankfully had thought of the excuse that I was on a new allergy medicine to pass on the round of champagne Caroline had ordered.

Her eyes had narrowed at me for a second but then nodded her head. I had seen Brantley smirking at me out of the corner of my eye on that one. I laid my head on his arm as he was laughing at something Thomas was saying when I felt my arm yanked. I turned to see Caroline nodding her head towards one of the cabanas near us. I trailed after her walking beside Britt. We followed her in and I shut the door sitting down quickly on a longue chair because I felt dizzy.

"Ok, so which one of you is going first and tell me?" Caroline asks with hands on her hips and a gleam in her eye.

"Huh?" I asked playing confused.

"Tell," Brittany squeaked. "There's nothing to tell."

"I call bullshit," Caroline said with a evil grin narrowing her eyes pointing a finger between the two of us. Then she gasped covering her mouth as tears welled up. "Both of you are pregnant aren't you!"

"Shhh Caroline," Brittany hissed waving her hand around for Caroline to lower her voice. I knew it, I thought. "Yes, I just found out. I'm not but a few weeks. We have been trying."

"I knew it," Caroline said with a laugh clapping her hands. "If you slide one more drink over to Jason to cover for you, we are gonna have to pack his ass out of here. And it won't be because he over celebrated winning Entertainer of the Year. Cass, want to share with the class?"

"Yes," I said blushing a little. "Yes I am. Happy now Caroline. We were waiting until I was a little farther along to tell everyone. Ours was a big oops."

"Yes!" Caroline squealed jumping up and down. Lord, the tequila was hitting her hard. "I'm gonna have babies to spoil! Cass, we gotta get you down the aisle quick. Sure you don't want to take this party to one of the chapels?"

"I'm sure Caroline," I growled closing my eyes. I was so going to have to lay down soon. "We will figure something out. But Vegas tonight is not going to be it."

"Ok ok," Caroline huffed then smirked at me. "That growl sister, starting to sound like BG."

"Am not," I huffed crossing my arms over my chest. I moaned as I felt another wave of nausea pass. I covered my mouth willing myself to not puke. "Caroline, go get B, please."

"On it," she said squeezing my shoulder as she headed back out into the party. Brittany sat down beside me rubbing my back in sympathy. I heard a rustle and she pushed a small pack of crackers into my hand.

"Here," she said. "I've found that these help."

"Thanks Britt," I said shaking my head. "But they won't. I've tried. It's been so bad I have to take medicine to keep anything down most days."

"Damn honey," Brittany murmured as I sighed closing my eyes. "That's not fun at all. Mine comes and goes. Jay, bless his heart, just stands there knowing its nothing he can do."

"Brantley has been a big help," I said with a soft smile. "Makes sure I take the medicine when I'm supposed and makes sure I eat. But other than that, I know he feels helpless. And we all know that right there drives him nuts."

"You are almost done with the final season right?" Brittany asked as I nodded.

"Yes," I said biting my lip and closing my eyes again. "Thank the Lord. If I am not sick, I've been tired and I only just found out week before last."

The door opened a moment later as Caroline came walking back in with Brantley on her heels. She gave me a soft smile. I guess I really was that pale.

"It gets better," she said looking at Britt and I both. "It really does."

"Sure hope so," I mumbled as Brantley stepped forward and squatted down in front of me lifting my chin up to get me to look at him. "Because I feel like hell."

"Ok baby girl," he murmured standing up holding a hand out for mine pulling me up gently. "Meds are wearing off aren't they."

"Yes," I answered as he tucked me into his side. "I'm feeling sick again and just so damn sleepy."

"Yep, upstairs for you," Brantley said leading me to the door tipping his hat at Caroline and Brittany. "Goodnight ladies. Have a feeling I will be seeing both of you at the house next week."

"Damn right," Caroline said with a wink. "Got a wedding to plan."

We walked out making our way inside to the elevator. I followed Brantley into the elevator as he leaned against the side pushing the button and I laid my head his chest.

"Our child," I mumbled into his shirt. "Is being an asshole right now."

He let out a deep laugh pulling me closer kissing my cheek.

"Did you expect anything different honey? I am the father and you my darlin can be a stubborn hard headed ass when you want to be baby."

"I'm not being stubborn about this," I grumbled.

"Oh yes you are woman," he chuckled rubbing his hands softly on my back making me arch closer. Damn, he smelled so good. I just wish I wasn't so damn tired. "Am I going to have to follow you to the set next week to make sure your ass eats like you are supposed to instead of going turkey hunting?"

"I'm not a damn child Brantley Keith," I growled pulling my head back to glare at him. He met my glare head on. "Don't even think about cancelling your trip. I know you have been looking forward to it and Cam is so damn excited."

"Gonna take care of yourself then sweetheart?" he asked as the elevator stopped on our floor. I stepped out ahead of him shaking my head.

"Yes," I snapped. Then a thought crossed my mind as we stepped into the quiet hall. I turned poking a finger into his chest. "I'm going to have a damn babysitter, aren't I?"

"Well baby," Brantley drawled trying to look innocent. "I may have mentioned something to PJ and he said he felt like playing TV star while I was gone. Drive you around. Make sure you eat. Funny as hell the other day when he took one look at you and knew you were pregnant."

"Dammit B," I whined stomping my foot as he unlocked the door holding it open for me. "I can do all that myself. I'm not a child, nor am I made of fine china!" I felt dizzy as I walked in the door and swayed a little on my feet. He caught my arm guiding me over to the bed.

"Yep, uh ok, I hear you," he said shaking his head. "Bed for you."

"Dammit," I growled glaring at him as I sank down onto the soft bed. "Have I told you I hate it when you are right?"

"Yes mam," Brantley said with a chuckle as he sank down to a knee by the side of the bed picking up one of my feet. "I think you have mentioned it a time or two over the years."

He slipped one heel off then the next massaging the arch of my foot making me sigh as my eyes got heavier. I swear, if I wasn't tossing my cookies I was sleepy. He stood up kissing my forehead before disappearing in the bathroom as I slipped the jewelry off and unpinned my hair letting it hang loose. I sat the stuff on the nightstand as he came walking back out with a wash cloth that he passed to me. I started slowly wiping off the makeup as he dug in his suitcase coming up with a t-shirt a second later.

"Come here Cass," he said softly helping me stand up as I turned for him to unzip the back of the dress making me sigh in relief. This one wasn't uncomfortable I was just ready to be out of it. Brantley slipped his t-shirt over my head before reaching around me to tug the covers down then pointing at me.

I crawled in as he settled them around me. Through cracked eyes I watched him grab a bottle of water and my medicine out of my bag then sat down beside me handing them to me. I gave him a grateful smile as I took the medicine handing the water bottle back to him. I settled my head against the pillows instantly feeling even sleepier. I barely registered him curling up beside me a minute later as I snuggled back against his chest falling into a deep sleep.

Brantley's POV

I felt Cassie stir against me as she sighed in her sleep making me blink my eyes open. She let out a small whimper then settled her head on my shoulder. I had made sure the blinds were pulled last night before I went to bed hoping she would be able to sleep as much as she could. I knew the fatigue and nausea were part of pregnancy but still didn't stop me from worrying about her.

I kissed her forehead softly as I played with the ends of her dark hair watching her sleep. I was being a little overprotective of her I knew, but I just didn't want anything to happen to her or the baby. I was thrilled that she was almost done with the show, so she could be on the road with us. She needed the down time more than she realized.

I prayed that when her off time was up she would balance things a little better. I knew I would do my damnedest to make sure she did. I slowly slipped my hand between us to rest my hand on her stomach smiling. I was equal parts excited and terrified about being a dad. I had been ready for kids the last couple of years, just hadnt been able to convince Cassie to slow down and marry me.

I still even after all these years don't think she understood just how much I loved her. I had just thought I had been in love before until I met her. Knowing she was it for me is the main reason I had waited her out. And before long it wouldn't just be the two of us anymore.

"You know," I heard mumbled and glanced down at Cassie laying there with her eyes still closed. "It's creepy as hell when you stare at me while I am sleeping."

"Well, " I murmured rolling to my side and kissing her softly. "It is the only time you look like an angel."

"Thanks," she growled cracking an eye open to glare at me. "Love you too ass."

"How are you feeling baby?" I asked brushing the hair away from her face as she snuggled closer.

"I'm scared to move," she said tracing a finger on my chest. "Don't feel sick right now but know as soon as I move."

"Maybe not," I said rubbing her stomach. She let out a giggle as I pushed the covers and slid down even with her stomach pushing my t-shirt up pressing a kiss right above her belly button before speaking. "Ok little one, do me a favor take it easy on your Mama today. She's been pretty sick. I promise to make sure she never grounds you if you will give her a break today."

"Good luck with that," Cassie said with a laugh dragging her nails over my short hair. "They are half you and half me. Face, it they are going to be stubborn and hard headed."

"You do have a point," I said with a laugh sitting up and leaning over to kiss her softly. "I do know this though."

"What's that B?" she asked smiling up at me.

"I can't wait to meet he or she," I whispered as she rubbed a hand along my cheek. God, I loved this woman.

"Me either," Cassie whispered back smiling widely.

It's the Little Things

- -

Cassie's POV

I reached up to straighten my messy bun as I bounced my leg up and down under the table. We had wrapped on the season yesterday with interviews with the cast today. Since they had taken the photos for the interview yesterday, I had dressed for comfort today in a thin green oversize long sleeve shirt that slipped off one shoulder with black workout leggings.

PJ had snickered and commented that I looked like I was ready to spend the day watching TV when I had walked out the door this morning as he handed me a muffin with an extra large Sprite. To say that he and Brantley were teaming up against me was an understatement. Yesterday had been such a long day that I had fallen asleep before we even pulled out of the studio lot. I pasted a smile on my face as the magazine rep turned her attention towards me after talking to Josh.

"Cassie, she said tossing her long blonde hair over her shoulder. I felt my stomach roll at the movement. "We all hear that congratulations are in order again. You and Brantley Gilbert are engaged again."

"Yes Ashley, we are," I said with a soft smile holding my left hand up.

"There's been a lot of speculation since you two spilt a few years back of whether you were still together or not," Ashley said narrowing her eyes at me. "Care to shed a little light on that."

I swallowed deeply against a wave of nausea and placed my hand on my stomach rubbing lightly since the table blocked anyone's view. Please, please little one don't make Mama sick right now. Brantley and I both had agreed that if the question was asked we would answer honestly.

"For about a year after we called things off," I said taking a deep breath. "we didn't see each other or speak. Then we ran into each other again at a night out with mutual friends. Since then we have done our best with our busy schedules. But I am taking some time off since the show is over and touring with him."

"Any wedding plans?" Ashley questioned with a grin. I smiled back in return. Sure, I want to answer, as soon as I can stop puking long enough I will be right on that.

"We have looked at a few dates," I answered as I started to feel slightly dizzy. Thank god I was sitting down. I had eaten and taken my medicine like I was supposed to. What was the deal. "Leaning towards something this fall if I can get him out of the woods long enough."

"Well I will say this," Ashley said fanning herself. "That was a hell of a way to announce an engagement. Last time you two just released a joint statement. This time, oh wow. That was some kiss then the look on people's faces when they noticed the ring."

"Yea," I said with a laugh. "I think B's exact words were just to let the ring do the talking."

"Got the job done," she said laughing with me as Josh winked over at me. I squeezed my hands together under the table as another wave of dizziness washed over me. I could see PJ narrowing his eyes as he watched me from the corner of the room.

"Well Cassie, Josh, thank you so much for sitting down with me. Anxious to see what happens with your characters in the finale. Cassie, congrats again on your engagement. You and BG look so happy together."

We both thanked her as she walked out of the room. Josh cut his eyes at me as the door shut with a quiet click as I laid my head down on the cool table.

"Cass," he said laying a hand on my shoulder." Are you ok?"

"No," I whispered closing my eyes against the spinning world. I felt like I was getting sick so I stood up quickly. I made a half step before losing my balance as Josh's hand shot out to grab me.

"PJ!" he yelled as I heard running footsteps as they both caught me. My head felt like it weighed a ton. "What's wrong with her?"

"She's pregnant," PJ mumbled then glared at Josh over the top of my head making him take a step back. "But so help me if you breathe a word of this, you will have to deal with me and BG."

"Mum is the word PJ," Josh said shaking his head then looking down at me. "She's so damn pale."

"Ok darlin," PJ said scooping me up. "To the hospital with you. I'll call your doctor on the way."

"PJ," I whined. "I'm fine. I just need sleep. Just take me to the house. All I want is sleep. And B. I want B."

"Oh, something tells me he will be showing up and soon," Josh said with a laugh as he opened the door to the side of the building as PJ handed over his truck keys for him to unlock the door. The whole cast and crew was so damn used to PJ hovering around the last few years when he wasn't out with Brantley.

I stretched out in the back seat my eyes closing as soon as I laid my head down. I could hear PJ on the phone as he pulled out of the lot. I just wanted to curl up and sleep for days.

Brantley's POV

I stalked through the hospital in Athens my heart pounding in my chest. I had been almost to the Georgia state line when PJ called me telling me he had left the studio lot headed to the hospital with Cassie. We had cut our trip short since Cam had gotten sick this morning and Eli had headed back with him. I could see stares as I quickened my pace hurrying down the hall looking for the room they had put her in.

I knew it was the head to toe camo with the exception of my backwards black hat. The face paint Cam had talked me into this morning that I had forgotten to wash off before I left the farm wasn't helping their stares any. I skidded to a halt as I saw the room and pushed the door open making PJ whirl around narrowing his eyes and putting a finger to his lips.

"Shh..." he grumbled. "She finally just went to sleep."

"Don't you shush me," I growled pointing towards a sleeping Cassie curled up under the blankets. Her normally tan skin was pale against the pillow. "That's my woman and my child."

"And I'm in charge of protecting them when you aren't around," PJ said walking back over to the chair to sit down as I sat on the edge of the bed with a sigh.

I lifted my hand to push a strand of hair off her cheek. I could see the shadows under her eyes and my heart sank. She was ok I hoped. I knew she had been getting sick a lot and I felt so damn powerless on not being able to help it was driving me nuts.

"I know," I mumbled the worry eating me up. "Just worried about her man. She's been taking her medicine and eating, hasn't she? I've only been gone a couple of days."

"Yes Boss," PJ growled then lowered his voice as Cassie stirred in her sleep reaching a hand out to thread her fingers with mine. "Just like she is supposed to. She's pushed herself a little more than either of us would have liked the last couple of days trying to get things finished. She's been asleep before we even have been a mile away from the set the last couple of nights."

"I sent you with her to make sure she didn't run herself ragged!" I snapped running a hand down my face in frustration as PJ narrowed his eyes at my tone. I knew I was probably out of line but I was so fucking worried. "Dammit PJ! I knew I should have cancelled this trip. She made sure I went because of Cam. I just knew she wouldn't slow down."

"BG," PJ growled crossing his arms and leaning forward in the chair. "I did everything I could to make sure she didn't overwork herself. The only reason she pushed was because she was trying to get done with it all, so she'd be ready to leave with us next week. In all the time y'all have been together she's never gotten to go for more than a handful of dates at a time."

"Both of y'all shut up," Cassie mumbled making us both swing our heads around to look at her.

"Last time I checked you jackasses I was a grown woman not a two-year-old."

"Sorry baby," I said leaning over to gently kiss her forehead. She blinked those beautiful chocolate brown eyes open to look up at me. PJ stood up to look at her over my shoulder.

"How you feelin now darlin?" he asked giving her a soft smile. Those two had instantly bonded from the beginning. He had reminded me several times before we started dating that I needed to get my shit together and man up when it came to Cassie.

"Like hell," she whispered biting her lip as she held her hand up with the IV. But this is supposed to be helping. "I just want my bed."

"Well sweetheart," I said with a quiet chuckle squeezing her hip. "As soon as the give me the ok to spring you from this joint I will take you there."

I leaned closer to her, narrowing my eyes as she struggled to keep her eyes open. "And that is where your sassy little ass is gonna stay unless it's to climb on the bus and then you better get comfortable in the bed on there. I'm not letting you out of my sight more than I have to."

"B," she whimpered shaking her head lightly. "It's just morning sickness."

"Actually," I heard from the doorway turning to see Dr. Nanda standing there with a look on her face. She had reminded Cassie at her checkup that as busy as she was she had to stay on top of things. "It's a little more than that."

"She ok?" I asked nervously lacing my fingers with Cassie's as the doctor patted my shoulder reassuringly.

"With a little time," she said looking at her notes. "Cassie's weight is still a little less than I would like it to be. I know you eat honey before you even start fussing. But as busy as you've staid you work it right back off. I'm officially diagnosing you with Hyperemisis gravidarum. Only few people experience it. Which is why the dizziness, nausea all the time and fatigue. We will keep with the meds you are already on. Lots and lots of fluids, five to six small meals a day, which is something from what PJ here has told me, you haven't been keeping up with, and lots of rest."

I stood up crossing my arms over my camo shirt and glaring down at Cass as she sunk back further into the pillows hanging her head.

"So what you are saying Dr. Nanda and let me make sure I have it all," I grumbled still glaring. "Is this extreme morning sickness not everyone gets. Cass is going to need more rest than a normal pregnant woman, five to six small meals, lots of fluids, nausea meds. Well, I can gurandamntee you, she will get it."

I shook a finger at Cassie making her meet my glare head on. Sick as a dog and still being stubborn as hell.

"She will get it even if I have to tie her stubborn hardheaded ass to the bed!"

"Brantley Keith," Cassie growled trying to sit up but struggled as a wave of dizziness hit her. PJ took hand and gently pushed her shoulder making her settle back against the bead as we glared at each other.

"I'll do what she says. But no way in hell are you tying me to the bed you damn caveman! I can still travel right?"

"Yes," Doctor Nanda told her with a kind smile. "As long as you rest. I know that touring can be just as hectic as filming but take naps when you can. Neither of you hesitate to call me if something is wrong. I can recommend someone near you at the time or work you in if y'all are home. But rest, rest, rest."

"Oh, she will," PJ and I both chimed making Dr. Nanda laugh. Cassie flipped both of us off weakly then shook her head.

"See," she grumbled. "I couldn't not nap even if I wasn't so tired all the time. My wardens here would make sure of it."

"Damn straight you are a gonna nap missy, "PJ said giving me a look.

"That's right," I said leaning down to kiss her softly. "We are gonna make sure you do everything Doc says baby girl. You are carrying our baby but more important than that is you being okay."

"Ok," she whispered leaning her head against my shoulder. We heard the door open and a tech came in wheeling an ultra sound machine.

"That IV is almost finished Cassie," Dr. Nanda said moving to make room. "I wanted to get a quick ultrasound before I let you go to make sure little one is doing ok."

"That's my cue," PJ said standing up from the chair. Cassie lifted her head to look at him as he dropped a kiss on her cheek then squeezed my shoulder. "Don't pass out Boss."

"I'm not gonna pass out you jackass," I growled making him let out a loud booming laugh. "Thanks PJ. Look I was out of line earlier man and I am sorry. I know there's only so much you can do to make her stubborn ass listen. I was just scared man."

"No worries Boss," he said with a smirk walking to the door. "We are good. She's a handful we all know that."

"Am not!" Cassie muttered then let out a hiss as the tech spread the gel onto her stomach. I gave her a grin earning me a glare as I pulled up the chair beside her bed. I sat down and threaded my fingers through hers as Dr. Nanda got started. After a minute, she turned her head to smile at both of us.

"Alright Mom and Dad," she said pointing at the screen. "There is your little one."

Cassie covered her mouth with her free hand as she gasped squeezing my hand tight. I saw the tears slipping down her cheeks as my own eyes started to water. Dr. Nanda took a couple of pictures before turning a knob. I heard a whoosh then a rapid thumping sound as I leaned forward in my chair closer to Cassie listening.

"That's the heartbeat," Dr. Nanda said grinning at us. "A good strong one too. Little one is doing great and measuring at eight weeks. I'll print you both out a couple copies of the ultrasound."

I vaguely nodded my head staring at the screen. I felt a soft hand on my cheek as Cassie turned my head slightly to look at her. Cass wiped a tear off my cheek with her thumb as she looked at me.

"You ok?" she asked giving me a watery smile.

"Yea baby," I answered softly staring at her. "More than ok." I pointed a finger at the screen my hand trembling slightly. "We did that. Us. We did that."

"Yes, we did," Cassie said kissing me gently then burrowing her head in my shoulder sighing. "Yes, we did."

Them Boys

B rantley's POV

I grabbed the last two bags off the floor in the foyer and handed them over to Tony to toss in my room on the bus and turned to holler up the stairs.

"Cassie!" I yelled. "We've got to go honey!"

"Coming!" she called back and a second later she appeared at the top of the stairs in a pair of leggings and one of my t-shirts. Sylo hot on her heels. Kolby was on his way to get him. I saw how pale she looked as she made it to the bottom of the stairs stopping near me. She had been home from the hospital for a week. The few interviews that she had needed to wrap up before we got back on the road for the summer leg of the tour she had been doing by phone or Skype.

"Feeling ok?" I asked reaching over to squeeze her hip.

"Just a little tired," she said with a sigh reaching down to rub the top of Sylo's head. I turned around putting my back to her and squatted down a little. I heard her let out a laugh as I looked at her over my shoulder.

"Well hop on baby girl," I said with a grin as she wrapped her arms around my neck and I reached back to boost her up wrapping her legs around my waist. I motioned my hand for Sylo to follow us as I headed to the door. Cassie propped her chin on my shoulder and I could see her grinning out of the corner of my eye.

I don't think she knew just how excited I was about her being on the road with us. Yea, she had come out for shows over the years. But it was never more than two in a row before she had somewhere she had to be. Kolby pulled up about the time we made it to the bus. He looked at Cassie on my back and rolled his eyes laughing as he climbed out of his truck.

"Taxi cab now bro?" he said with a grin kissing Casss cheek. I shrugged my shoulders bouncing her a little then flinched when she smacked the back of my head. Yea, might not be the best idea in the world to jostle the nauseous pregnant woman.

"Hey what she wants she gets," I said with a snicker. I let out a yelp when Cassie grabbed my ear then leaned over to kiss my cheek.

"Don't let the teddy bear fool you Kolbs," she said with a giggle. "He offered."

"Lord," Kolby said rolling his eyes. "You two can be so sickeningly sweet sometimes it makes my teeth hurt."

"Get used it Kolbs!" Cassie said shaking her head as I walked over turning around to set her on the steps. Kolby pushed me over and wrapped Cassie in a tight hug. She squeezed him back kissing his cheek before he stepped away. "We'll only be gone two weeks Kolbs. You have this look on your face."

"I know Cass," he said rubbing the back of his neck. "One you looked like you needed it and two, well way things have been in the past I just never knew."

"I'm here for good," Cassie said giving him a soft smile as I gave my brother a hug. "I'm not going anywhere. Even when he gets tired of me. I'll just got hide out at Mama's."

"I'll never get tired of you darlin," I said with a grin. "And the sooner I get a wedding band on your finger the better."

"What's the rush hotshot?" she said with a smirk and a wink. Kolby started laughing and motioned for Sylo to follow him to the truck as Cassie backed up the steps of the bus. I let out a low growl shaking my head stalking after her.

"What's the rush?" I grumbled glaring at her. The twinkle in her eyes told me she was playing and enjoying the look on my face. "Oh, I don't know honey, I've only been begging the last couple of years."

"Man, has got a point," Tony said shutting the doors behind me and earning a cuff to the shoulder from Cassie before I scooped her up laughing.

"See....." I drawled as the bus started to roll out and I shut the door then sat Cassie down gently on the couch. She grabbed my hand tugging me down beside her automatically settling her head on my shoulder as I stretched my legs out. "You know we are gonna have to tell the boys right?"

"I know," Cassie said propping her chest on my shoulder lacing her fingers with mine." Ben will get suspicious quick with you being more protective than normal. And PJ makes every step I do when you aren't around. I'm gonna want to shoot all of y'all before this tour is over."

"Now baby," I drawled poking my lip out at her. "I'm not that bad, am I?"

"Did you seriously just ask me that Brantley Keith?" she said with a loud laughing poking my chest.

"Okay, okay," I grumbled kissing the top of her head. "Maybe I am little protective. I just want you and little one to be safe."

"We are," she whispered smiling up at me her eyes getting heavy. "We are."

Cassie's POV

"Baby," I heard Brantley whisper shaking my arm gently. "We are here. You coming with me to do sound check?"

"Yea," I said blinking my eyes open sitting up slowly. The wave of dizziness passed pretty quickly. I held a hand up at Brantley who was staring down at me with a concerned look on his face. "I'm fine, I promise."

"You sure?" he asked skeptically pulling me to my feet gently. I stood on tip toes kissing his cheek.

"Yes B," I sighed. "I am fine. I just sat up too fast."

"Okay," he murmured wrapping an arm around me as we walked down the bus steps. I glanced around at all the activity going on and got a little excited. I had missed being around all the flurry involved in getting things set up for a show. The energy. B was usually bouncing around, but he was more concerned with keeping an eye on me than. We were a few steps from the bus when I heard my name called. I glanced over to see Ben jogging towards us with the rest of the band behind him.

"Cassie!" he yelled. I gave him a big grin as he got closer. Ben grabbed me around my waist picking me up swinging me around. I let out a yelp as I heard Brantley and PJ both yell "Ben! Put her down!"

"What the hell guys?" Ben complained coming to a stop squeezing me tight. I loved my cousin. He was just like my brother, but right now I was about to kill him. That was if I didn't puke on him first. "Calm your tits!"

I smacked his shoulder trying to get his attention as he glared at Brantley and PJ.

"Ben," I mumbled smacking him a little harder. "Beeennnnn!"

"Unless you want her to puke on you man," Brantley grumbled shaking his head. "You may want to put her down."

I slapped a hand over my mouth as Ben pulled back to look at me with wide eyes sitting me down on my feet. I bit the inside of my cheek praying I didn't hurl in front of everyone.

"Shit Cass," Ben said putting a hand on my arm to steady my shaking legs. "What is wrong?"

Out of the corner of my eye I could see Brantley and PJ both trying to get to me as my eyes rolled back in my head and the world faded to black.

Brantley's POV

I felt my heart stop as Cassie started to faint and I pushed Ben out of the way to catch her as she started to fall. I knew I should have gotten her to stay on the bus. She had been up early this morning to wrap up the last couple of interviews she needed to do before we got on the road. I hadn't argued with her as long as she got some rest throughout the day. I scooped her up and strode towards the bus with her with the guys trailing behind me.

"What the hell is wrong with her BG?" Jesse asked his voice laced with concern. I knew they all were freaking out because none of them knew what was going on. I shot Ben a glare over my shoulder as I walked up the steps of the bus and over to the couch. I gently laid Cassie down then kneeled at her side with my hand on her cheek. She had done this the other day scaring the shit out of me. Was only for a couple of minutes but still worried me.

"BG," Ben asked quietly. I could hear the tremble in his voice. I knew he was worried. "What the hell is wrong with her?"

"She's pregnant," I growled stroking her cheek then cut my eyes back at him.

"She's what?" he asked letting out a gasp. "Shit and I was swinging her around. She okay? The baby okay? Don't you fucking think that was something yall should have told us!"

"We were going to ass," I snarled then whipped my head back around as I felt Cassie stir. I smoothed the hair off her forehead giving her a soft smile.

"Calm down Bennie Boo," she murmured blinking her eyes open. "I'm fine. Have to take a little more care than a normal pregnant woman, but I am fine. No more swinging me around though ok. As long as I eat and take the medicine for the nausea, I am ok. And trust me, B and PJ have been on my ass about it."

"Damn right you are gonna be," Ben growled crossing his arms and narrowing his eyes at her. I smothered a laugh at the evil glare she gave him back. She hated all the coddling she had been getting but well, tough shit.

"Fuck," Cassie whined sitting up slowly and leaning her head against the back of the couch. "Dammit y'all I am a grown woman. I can take care of myself."

"Uh huh sure you can," Ben snapped. "We've all seen how run down you will let yourself get when you are filming. Well, now you aren't, and you now have baby Gilbert on board, you damn sure are going to take care of yourself."

"So, freaking unfair," she said poking her lip out making me chuckle. I laughed even harder when the guys chimed in.

"Tough shit," they all grumbled crossing their arms glaring at her. Well I'll be, the rest of this tour was gonna be interesting.

"Enjoy this shit now," she growled pointing a finger at all of them. "Because when this shit passes, you are all in for it. PJ?"

"Yes, Little Mama?" PJ said with a smirk looking at her.

"Bring me my wooden spoon," she said with an evil grin. "Mama taught me a new trick on how to rap them knuckles really good."

"Aww shit," Jesse said as the boys started backing off the bus slowly. "Time for sound check."

Ben shot her a soft smile then darted off the bus following the rest of them. Those two would bump heads over this more than me and her because they were so much alike. PJ followed after them with a booming laugh.

I tugged Cassie's hand pointing at the couch for her to lay back down. She gave me a sigh then stretched out. I leaned over to place a soft kiss on her stomach making her giggle before I pulled back and stood up leaning down to brush my lips on hers.

"Rest darlin," I murmured kissing her cheek." I will come back and get you when we get done."

"Okay," she whispered getting comfortable." I'm getting tired of being tired all the time B."

"I know baby," I said draping her fuzzy UGA blanket over her. "But you are growing a little human. That's a tough job."

"How come its so tough for me?" she grumbled closing her eyes and sighing.

"I wish I knew sweetheart," I said kissing her forehead. "I'd give anything to be the one sick instead of you."

She grinned up at me opening her eyes and putting a hand on my cheek. "That's sweet baby," she said with a quiet laugh. "But I wouldn't wish that on you, trust me. BG nation would be a little disappointed if you were too busy hurling instead of bouncing around on that stage. Now, go get soundcheck over."

I gave her one more kiss then headed to the door of the bus. I looked back before I headed down the steps noting that she had already dozed off. Good, she needed all the rest she could get.

I'm Comin Over

- -

Cassie's POV

I checked my reflection in the mirror on more time then stepped out of the bathroom looking for my shoes to put on. I had on just a plain hot pink t-shirt with my cut off blue jean shorts. But knowing how much a certain someone loved these shorts, made me feel like a million bucks. I grabbed my Converses and a pair of socks before padding to the front of the bus to put them on.

Brantley was in the middle of doing an interview before the show. I couldn't help but smile a little because I felt better than I had in a couple of weeks. I rubbed a hand across my stomach praying that it would last. I wanted to enjoy the show tonight. I would have loved to have watched it from the pit because it had been years, but I knew better than to even bring it up to my two guard dogs. I was tying my shoe when I heard a knock at the door before PJ walked in. He gave me a cautious look as he crossed his arms leaning against the cabinet.

"Feeling okay Cass?" he asked.

"Yea," I said finishing up and standing to grab my phone. "I actually really do. I want to enjoy tonight while it lasts. Yes, before you ask, I took a nap, ate something before B left for VIP, and took my meds."

"Good," PJ said with a wink. "Well your chariot awaits madam."

I barked out a loud laugh slipping my pass around my neck and following him off the bus to the golf cart. We made our way to the venue and I leaned back against the seat smiling.

"Good to see that smile darlin," PJ said as he maneuvered around the eighteen wheelers.

"Me too," I said with a happy sigh. "I feel better than I have in a while. Glad to know the only schedule I need to try and keep up with is Brantley's. I still have to do a couple of remote interviews but thats after the finale next week and I told Marsha I would do them at my own pace."

"Good to hear," he said parking then jogging around to hold a hand out to me. "She needed a foot put down on her a long time ago."

"I know," I said standing up. I bit my lip looking up at PJ. "She's already pouting about the time off, she's really gonna flip when I tell her I'm pregnant. I had told the show producer so he could alter a few scenes but that was it. My contract with her is almost up. I was thinking of talking to Rich next week when he comes in to catch a show about representing me too. I know he deals more with the music business but he's always been the accommodating one when it came to matching our schedules."

"Best idea I have heard in a long time," PJ said with a laugh holding a big arm out for me to hold onto as he headed inside. "She was never a big fan of Boss anyhow. Thought you needed to attach yourself to a Hollywood pretty boy. Woman did not get that was not your type."

"Nope," I said with a laugh. "I prefer my outlaw biker country boy from GA who writes songs about me."

"That's the truth," he said grinning as we found the guys huddled up back stage getting ready to go on. "That man was head over heels the first time his stubborn ass laid eyes on you."

"That I was," Brantley said with a smirk wrapping an arm around my waist pulling me into his side. I bowed my head as Jesse said the prayer. They all stopped to drop a kiss on my cheek before heading to take their places on stage as the opening music started. I stood on tip toe giving Brantley a deep kiss making him pull his head back with a gasp.

"Well," he said with a chuckle. "Someone seems to be feeling better."

"Yes I am," I said with a grin pressing closer to him. "Better than I've felt in a while."

He leaned down kissing me again flicking his tongue against mine as I fisted my hand in his t-shirt tugging him closer.

"Mmmm....." Brantley said with a chuckle. "I'll have to remember that."

"You better," I murmured. "Kick ass hot shot."

"Yes mam," he said with a wide grin before jogging to take his place. "Always do!"

I walked over to my stool that PJ had pulled out and settled down to watch the show. I felt a wide grin spread across my lips as I watched Brantley appear from the middle of the stage. He had the time of his life anytime he was up there. I was so proud of him. I settled a hand over my still flat stomach and felt my eyes tear up slightly.

Yea, I may be feeling like hell most days, but I knew when I held this little one in my arms the first time it would be all worth it. I tapped my foot and sang along with the songs. I had missed this. I loved watching the guys play. My eyes narrowed a little when Brantley turned to look over at me as he handed his guitar off to a roadie with a wide grin.

"Alright y'all," he said with a laugh. "As you know I recently got, hell how would you put it, reengaged I guess. I'm sure a lot of you have heard of the lovely Miss Cassie Paige. Cass, can you come here?"

I narrowed my eyes at him before slipping off my stool and stepping carefully over the wires making my way onto the stage with a wave as I came into view of the crowd. Brantley wrapped an arm around me and kissed my cheek. I sooo didn't like the shit eating grin on his face. I pinched his side as he looked down at me.

"Well," Brantley said giving me a wink and looking out at the crowd." I thought I would do something tonight since shes out on the road with us for the rest of the tour. I will admit this lady knows she has songs about her on the last two albums and she may kill me for this one but I guess it has described us the last few years so I thought I would borrow it. "

He threaded his fingers through mine as Ben kicked off the song. I cocked an eyebrow at him as he started to sing then shook my head as I recognized the song. This man, sometimes I swear.

We say goodbye, see you around

We turn our backs then turn back around

We break up, we make up and we make love

We cant seem to let go girl

So Im comin' over

Runnin' every red light

To Hell with the closure

Save it for another time

Try not to think about you

But it aint workin'

Why put out a fire when its still burnin'

Just when I think movin' on is gettin' closer

Im comin' over

Im all alone, but youre on my phone

Tellin' me you miss me and that youre at home

Who knows what we are in the mornin'

All I know is I want you

So Im comin' over

Runnin' every red light

To Hell with the closure

Save it for another time

Try not to think about you

But it aint workin'

Why put out a fire when its still burnin'

Just when I think movin' on is gettin' closer

Im comin' over

Oh I'm comin' over

Yeah we said that were done and I know that its late

But you already know, Im on my way

Im comin' over

Runnin' every red light

To Hell with the closure

Save it for another time

Try not to think about you

But it aint workin'

Why put out a fire thats burnin'

Im comin' over

Runnin' every red light

To Hell with the closure

Save it for another time

Try not to think about you

But it aint workin'

Why put out a fire when its still burnin'

Just when I think movin' on is gettin' closer

Im comin' over

Oh I'm comin' over

He gave me a smirk as he sang the last note looking at me. I couldn't help but smile shaking my head at him. I grabbed the middle of his t-shirt yanking his lips down to mine as he wrapped both arms around me bending me back slightly deepening it making the crowd roar. Brantley pulled back slightly looking down at me.

"I love you," he murmured giving me a heart stopping smile.

"I love you too," I said as he stood me back up on my feet. I gave him a wink as I turned to head back off stage. I felt a sharp pop on my ass as I heard him chuckle through his microphone.

"Let me tell y'all," he said as I walked away. "I am a very, very lucky man that she finally caved and agreed to marry me. Very lucky indeed."

Surprise: Part I

- -

Brantley's POV

I answered a quick text on my phone as I walked back down the hall to our bedroom. I chuckled when I looked up as I walked in at Cassie standing in front of the mirror on the closet door cussing under her breath as she tried to zip the back of her dress. Caroline had planned an engagement party for us while we were home for a week break.

She and Mama had been busy since we left two weeks ago. But they had wanted to do this and hadn't wanted Cassie to lift a finger. Cass had bitched at first then they both had glared at her shutting her up. We had already been taking bets on what month of her pregnancy she would kill Ben.

They had already been arguing like a pair of squabbling siblings and we were only a couple of weeks into the summer leg of the tour. He'd need body armor before it was all said and done. I did my best to run interference, so she didn't get herself too worked up.

"Need some help baby?" I asked smothering a grin as she sighed dropping her head in defeat as I walked up behind her.

"Yes," she grumbled with a big sigh covering her mouth as she yawned. "I'm still half asleep."

"Well you gotta wake up sweetheart," I said with a laugh as I zipped her white sundress up before placing a soft kiss on her bare shoulder. She had curled her long hair and left it to tumble around her tan shoulders. I wrapped my arms around her waist and met her eyes in the mirror as she leaned back against my chest. "You look beautiful as always Cass."

"Well you clean up pretty good yourself hotshot. You ready?" she asked with a soft smile making my grin widen. Mama had dug out one my black button up shirts and threatened to tan my hide if I so much as pulled out a pair of jeans with holes in them. Like the good son I am, I had listened. I had on a pair of dark colored jeans, the shirt she had put out but I had rolled the sleeves up my arms and had even left my hat off for now.

"Baby," I said with a loud laugh turning her around pulling her over to sit on the edge of the bed so I could help her pull her brown pointed toe boots on. She laughed as I sank to my knees and slipped the first one on. I have been ready. "Just been waiting on you darlin."

"Oh, you have huh," Cassie said with a giggle as I slipped the second boot on then stood up pulling her to her feet. I leaned down to brush a soft kiss across her lips then laced our fingers together tugging her towards the door.

"Yes, mam I have," I said with a big wink as we walked down the stairs. Caroline had kept it small as could be with just our family and friends. Cassie leaned her head on my arm as we walked to the back deck. I grinned down at her as we stopped and looked around. They had done a hell of a job of putting this party together.

I had laughed earlier when I had pulled up from running over to Mama's to get something she needed to see Caroline directing Til and Kolby on putting white lights in the trees around the back yard. She had arranged bundles of Cassie's favorite roses around the tables. I saw the dance floor Mama of all people had insisted on. I'll be honest, I couldn't wait to drag my beautiful fiancée out onto it later. Hey, I looked for any excuse to get my arms around her.

"It's beautiful," Cassie murmured looking around in awe. She looked up at me giving me a secretive smile as I patted the pocket of my shirt winking at her. I heard the door from the kitchen close and turned my head to see Caroline and Mama walking our way.

"Well," Mama said with a big smile leaning over to give us both a kiss on the cheek." You two ready to get this party started?"

"Mama you party animal you," I said with a chuckle earning me a smack in the arm." Just a minute. We've got one guest we are waiting on."

"I thought everyone was here," Caroline said shaking back her blonde hair narrowing her blue eyes in confusion. "I already told you Luke couldn't reschedule his interview. He's still fuming over it. Told Kerri if he had to miss this then no way in hell was he missing the wedding."

"Yea, umm poor Luke," Cassie said with a nervous laugh making Mama give her a funny look. I heard the door open and let out a sigh of relief. Mama turned her head to see who had walked out then gave me a look before turning to greet the last guest.

"Why Bro. Marks, I didn't realize the kids had invited you," Mama said as I held my hand out to shake his. He gave Mama a hug then leaned over to give Cassie one.

"Um..." he stumbled over what to say. "Yea it was a last minute idea Miss Becky."

"BG," Caroline growled crossing her arms narrowing her eyes at us. "What is going on?"

"Wanna tell them?" I asked Cassie looking down at her. She shrugged her shoulders as she grinned up at me. I put my fingers to my mouth letting out a loud whistle to get everyones attention. Kolby stopped mid stride to the food table thinking it was Mama busting him. Ben and Jesse stopped to look at us like we had went crazy. PJ had a shit eating grin on his face.

The conversations below us came to a halt as everyone stopped to look up at us. "Well, now that I have your undivided attention. Cass and I are both thankful and blessed to have our friends and family with us tonight. I know it's hard to get all of our schedules lined up to be in the same place at the same time. Which is why the masterminds that are Caroline and Mama threw this together for us." I gave them both a big smile before pulling Cassie closer looking down at her before speaking again. I almost stumbled over my words at the look in her eyes.

"That being said. I know y'all thought you were here for that long waited engagement party. Well, we decided to give you one even better. How about a wedding instead?"

"Are you serious?" I heard Mama ask making me tear my eyes from Cassie to look over at her. She had her mouth open in shock. Caroline was bouncing up and down clapping her hands.

"Finally!" Brittany and Lauren both yelled making me grin as Cassie shook her head. Mama tackled both of us in a hug.

"Thank the Lord," she murmured kissing both of us on the cheek. "Finally."

I looked down at Cassie giving her a soft smile.

"Ready for this baby girl?" I asked leaning down to look in her eyes. My smile grew wider as she placed a hand on my cheek nodding her head.

"Yep," she said with a smirk. "Been waiting on you hotshot."

"Knew I should have drug your ass to a chapel when we were in Vegas," I grumbled shaking my head.

"I tried to get you to remember," Caroline said from the side of us with a laugh.

"Yea well," Cassie snapped back with a laugh. "I like this idea much better. Knocking off all your socks. Be sure to record for Luke."

"Oh, I will," she said with a laugh walking down the steps to take a seat beside Mama. Lauren tossed a pack of tissues over to both of them with a laugh. I looked down at Cassie pulling her over to the top of the steps.

"I love you Cass," I said quietly squeezing her hands.

"Love you too B," she whispered back with a soft smile making my whole world feel complete.

Surprise: Part II

- -

C assie's POV

I laced my fingers with Brantley's as he nodded at Bro. Marks to start the ceremony. I could hear sniffles from Mama Becky and Aunt Shelia and we hadn't even got started yet. I couldn't blame them though because as soon as I lifted my eyes to lock with Brantley's I felt my own water with tears.

I mentally kicked myself for waiting so damn long to get here. I pulled myself out of my thoughts when he tugged my hand slightly making me step closer as he gave me a concerned look. I squeezed his hand back to let him know I was okay.

"Dearly beloved," Bro. Marks said giving us a wide smile. "We are gathered here today to witness the joining of Brantley and Cassie. Even I will say what the rest of y'all are thinking, it's about time you two. "He gave us a wink as everyone else clapped and cheered." That being said, and I doubt there is anyone, if there is anyone who thinks these two should not be wed, speak now or forever hold your peace."

I turned my head slightly giving Kolby and Ben a sharp glare daring either of them to say a word thinking they are funny. I let out a small sigh of relief and looked back up at Brantley. I felt the hairs on the back of my neck stand up when I heard the door from the kitchen open and someone yell out.

"I object," a deep voice called. Brantley and I both let a growl out making the preacher jump. I was going to kill someone.... .slowly.

"I object," they said again as bootsteps approached us. "You two seriously didn't think you were getting married without me did you!"

"Thomas Luther Bryan," I snapped as Luke walked over with a big grin on his face." I will shoot you. "

"I'm just glad I made it in time," Luke said wrapping an arm around my shoulders kissing my cheek.

"Was scared I was going to miss this."

"Well," Brantley drawled giving him a playful glare." How about you get your hands off my wife and go grab yours."

"She's not your wife yet buddy," Luke said with a laugh as Brantley shoved his shoulder.

"Well I am trying to fix that," he growled tugging me closer to him making everyone laugh.

"Took you long enough," Luke called out over his shoulder as he walked down the steps.

"Now," Bro Marks said with a chuckle making me roll my eyes. "If we have that over with let's get on with it shall we. I have been blessed enough to get to know this pair over the years and there has never been two people better suited for each other. They love each other truly and deeply. It's a love that many strive their whole lives to find. It's something that shines through into everything that you do. I believe you have expressed wanting to say your own vows. Brantley, you may go ahead."

"Cassie," Brantley said softly looking down into my eyes. I felt my heart speed up at the love I could see shining in his green eyes. He lifted a hand cupping my cheek before clearing his throat and speaking again. "Baby, I was literally head over boots the first moment I laid eyes on you. I don't know what I ever did to deserve you, but I am so glad for it. I love you with all my heart and soul. You have seen me at my best. You have seen me at my worst. Cass, you know me better than anyone else in this world, yet you still manage to love me. Through my scars, faults and flaws, you love me for me. Thank you for loving the outlaw in me baby. You are my best friend and one true love. There is still a part of me, even standing here today that cannot believe that I'm the one who gets to marry you. I promise to love and stand by you always, until the day I take my last breath. I love you and I am thankful I get to spend the rest of my life showing you." He calmly lifted my left hand slipping the matching platinum and diamond band onto my ring finger.

"Cassie," Bro Marks says softly as I wipe at my eyes trying to remember the words I had carefully written early this morning when I couldn't sleep. I had curled up in the chair in the corner of our room watching Brantley sleep with a hand resting over my stomach in awe of the life I had been given.

Brantley wiped a tear away with his thumb then laced his fingers back with mine. I could hear the sniffles from the crowd at his words.

"Brantley," I said with a sigh making him smile." I have had the chance to play many roles in my career but God made sure I was steered towards my best and greatest one I will ever play and that is your wife. I choose you B. To stand by your side and sleep in your arms. To be the joy in your heart and food for you soul. To learn with you and grow with you even as time and life change us both. I vow to never get so busy again I lose sight of how much I love and need you.

I know that our lives can get hectic. I know that they can get busy, but I never want to live without you in my life again. You are the other half to my whole. I promise to respect you and cherish you as an individual, as my partner in all the things life will throw at us, because I know that we not only complete each other, but complement each other. There is no me without you.

May we have many adventures in this crazy whirlwind life of ours and I look forward to telling our grandchildren about it when we grow old together. Even if I didn't know it at the time, I have been yours from the very first moment we locked eyes and I will be yours until the day I die. I love you with all that I have to give."

With shaking hands, I lifted his left hand up to gently push the wide black band onto is finger with a soft smile.

I let out a surprised gasp when he leaned forward brushing his lips with mine causing everyone to laugh. Brantley broke this kiss with a deep chuckle as he lifted his head and I reached up to wipe a tear off his cheek with a watery smile.

"Jumping the gun just a little son," Bro Marks said with a laugh as Brantley shrugged his shoulders and grinned.

"Do you Brantley Keith Gilbert, promise to take Cassandra Nicole Paige as your lawfully wedded wife, to have and to hold, to love and cherish in sickness and in health as long as you both shall live?"

"I do," Brantley said with a wide grin at me.

"Do you Cassandra Nicole Paige, promise to take Brantley Keith Gilbert, as your lawfully wedded husband, to have and to hold, to love and cherish in sickness and in health as long as you both shall live?"

"I do," I said softly and smiled as Brantley stepped closer to me again with a light sheen of tears in his eyes.

"Well then," Bro Marks said rolling his eyes at Brantley. "By the power invested in me by the great state of Georgia, Brantley you may kiss your bride..again."

Brantley snaked an arm out to wrap around my waist tugging me against him with a wink.

"Finally," he murmured lowering his head and kissing me deeply. I felt my knees start to go weak as I dug my fingers into his shoulders try to stay upright. I let out a laugh as he broke the kiss rubbing his nose against mine smiling. "I've got you lock, stock, and barrel now Cass."

I heard Bro Marks start laughing loudly as everyone below us cheered.

"It is with great pleasure," he said laying a hand on each of our shoulders. "That I introduce to you for the first time Mr. and Mrs. Brantley Gilbert."

The Rest of My Life

Brantley's POV

I slipped my hand under the table to rest gently on Cassie's knee as I leaned over placing a soft kiss onto her cheek making her turn to smile at me before turning head to finish her conversation with Caroline and Brittany. We were all at a big table to the side of the make shift dance floor setup in our backyard as the sky grew darker. There where thousands of twinkling white lights reminding me of trees full of stars.

Luke smirked at me across the table as Caroline leaned her head against his shoulder. I flipped him off making him laugh. I owed the jackass for saying he objected. Fucker. Thomas had Lauren wrapped up out on the dance floor with Willa Gray between them. Damn, I was so ready for that.

Cassie and I were sitting the fence on finding out what we were having. It changed from day to day. Cassie slid her hand into mine as she turned to lean against me. I smiled at Jason over her and Britts heads as he shook his head at their discussion of babies. We were going to make the announcement in a couple of weeks. Let the news of our surprise wedding settle down some.

Cass looked up at me a few minutes later letting out a quiet giggle. She turned to put a hand on my cheek with a smile.

"What?" I murmured lowering my lips to brush gently against her. She hummed softly kissing me then pulled back with a wink.

"Still got a little bit of icing in your beard," Cassie said with a laugh as I jutted my chin out for her to brush it away. I tickled her lightly as she elbowed me.

"Well," I said rolling my eyes at her. "Shouldn't have tried to shove a piece of cake down my throat darlin."

"You asked for it hotshot," she said with a grin leaning over to nip my bottom lip. "You started it."

"Get a piece of that cake to go later baby," I whispered in her ear making her shiver. "May have plans for that icing."

"I like the way you think husband," Cassie said with a sly grin. I felt my heart speed up at her words.

Husband, fucking finally. I lifted her left hand kissing her rings softly feeling complete. I had the woman I loved as my wife finally. Anything else was just icing on the cake. I could never write another song, make another album, or do another tour and I would be okay. I had her and the addition to our family in the coming months. My life was full and complete. I would thank God everyday for the rest of my life for her.

I heard the familiar chords start and smiled down at Cassie before sliding my chair back and pulling her to her feet. Lacing our fingers together, I walked her out to the middle of the dance floor before wrapping my arms around her tightly to sway to the music. "Amazed" was our song. I saw Ben give me a wink as he walked away from the DJ table with a smile.

I nodded my head in thanks before resting my forehead on Cassie's as I looked into her warm eyes singing softly to her. She laid her hand on my chest playing with the buttons of my shirt as a light shimmer of tears gathered in her eyes.

"You okay baby girl?" I asked wiping one away with my thumb.

"Yes," Cassie said softly nodding her head. "Happy tears. I promise."

"Good," I said then kissed her gently. "I promise to do the best that I can to keep a smile on your face for the rest of our lives. I know I'll piss you off. I am a master at it after all. But you won't ever doubt just how much I love you Cass. Thank you for loving me and for being my wife."

"Nowhere else I would want to be B," Cassie said standing up on her tip toes melding her body to mine. "You are mine, all mine for the rest of our lives. I'm looking forward to all the adventures we are gonna have and memories we are gonna make."

"Well baby," I said stepping back and lacing my fingers with hers. "What do you say to sneaking out of here and getting started on those memories."

"Lead the way handsome," Cassie said slipping a hand into my back pocket. "I'd follow you anywhere."

THE END